The Disregarded Dragon

Table of Contents:

i.	**Playlist** – Page 3	xx.	**Chapter 17 – Kai:** Page 243
ii.	**Author's Warning** – Page 4	xxi.	**Chapter 18 – Nieves:** Page 250
iii.	**Preface** – Page 5	xxii.	**Epilogue – Conlaed:** Page 268
iv.	**Chapter 1 – Nieves Eirwen:** Page 6	xxiii.	**Bonus Chapter – Burning-Wind:** Page 272
v.	**Chapter 2 –** Nieves – Page 15	xxiv.	**Family Trees** – Page 250
vi.	**Chapter 3 – Kai Abeloth:** Page 33	xxv.	**Extras** – Page 277
vii.	**Chapter 4 – Kai:** Page 46	xxvi.	**Book 4 excerpt – Princess Kinley** – Page 285
viii.	**Chapter 5 – Nieves:** Page 61	xxvii.	**Books By Kristen Elizabeth** – Page 296
ix.	**Chapter 6 – Nieves:** Page 82	xxviii.	**Acknowledgments** – Page 299
x.	**Chapter 7 – Kai:** Page 99	xxix.	**About the Author** – Page 300
xi.	**Chapter 8 – Nieves:** Page 114		
xii.	**Chapter 9 – Nieves:** Page 126		
xiii.	**Chapter 10 – Kai:** Page 142		
xiv.	**Chapter 11 – Kai:** Page 156		
xv.	**Chapter 12 – Nieves:** Page 171		
xvi.	**Chapter 13 – Kai:** Page 189		
xvii.	**Chapter 14 – Nieves:** Page 202		
xviii.	**Chapter 15 – Kai:** Page 214		
xix.	**Chapter 16 – Nieves:** Page 220		

The Royal's Saga, Book 3: The Disregarded Dragon

Book 3 Theme: Queen of the North – Two Steps from Hell

Muse Playlist (Alphabetical Order)

1. Citizen Soldier - Unbreakable
2. Disturbed – The Curse
3. Disturbed – Serpentine
4. Ellie Goulding – Burn
5. Ellie Goulding – My Blood
6. Imagine Dragons – Thunder
7. Jonathan Young – Dark Horse cover/Katy Perry mashup
8. KAI theme: Warlord – Cavalera Conspiracy
9. Katy Perry – Firework
10. Korn – Coming Undone
11. Linkin Park – With You
12. Nickleback – Savin' Me
13. NIEVES theme: Epic Hopeful - Proluxestudio
14. Nightwish – Astral Romance
15. Papa Roach – Gettin' away with murder
16. Skillet – Whispers in the Dark
17. SR-71 – Tomorrow
18. System of a Down – Aerials
19. System of a Down – I-E-A-I-A-I-O
20. System of a Down – Revenga
21. Within Temptation – A Demon's Fate

Author's Warning:

This book contains trigger warnings and material, including:

Child Neglect
Child Abuse/bullying
Assault/gore/Murder
Kidnapping
Nonconsensual marriage
Mentions of minor rape/ rape/ attempted rape
Post Partum Depression
Attempted assault/ sexual harassment

These triggers can be found in the following chapters:
Preface, Chapters 1, 2, ***3**, 6, 8, **10**, 14, **16**, 18, Epilogue
(*chapters with hard triggers*)

Please proceed with caution, and if triggered by any of these themes or by the story, please seek the appropriate help or resources. Be safe! Thank you!

Preface

December, 721 Fire Drake Dynasty

I returned from the clearing in the forest, just outside of my dwelling...for the last time.

I took it as a strange omen, of sorts, to see one single red snapdragon flower in a field full of white ones in the middle of winter. It was as if my home was bidding me farewell, too.

"Did you hear?" I heard the maids whispering to the knights who loaded my few belongings into the carriage. "She's worthless to the young king, so she's being sent to tie us to another family instead! I guess that really *is* the only thing she is good for..."

"It is so sad that they wasted so many years taking such good care of her and waiting for her powers to arrive. She should have just disappeared when she passed the age of power..."

I can hear you, I thought, a little bitter.

Though, I can't bring myself to be angry. They were right, after all...

Chapter 1 – Nieves Eirwen

December, 721 Fire Drake Dynasty

I had just turned twelve years of age, in August of this year.

I was born in August of the year 709, Fire Drake Dynasty year.

Now, it had been an entire two years after my powers *should* have arrived.

Sadness froze the blood in my veins, and tears stung my eyes behind my black lace veil.

My father, the great king of the Northern kingdom in the Snow drake territory, had married my mother for her great beauty shortly after he had been widowed.

He had a son by his previous wife who was his heir to the throne of the north, and that son was *flawless*…but my mother had given him *me*, and I had been praised as the beautiful snow princess of the north…destined to become a powerful beauty, like my mother.

My mother, however, had passed away just shortly after birthing me. No one had known the cause, but they insisted that she had been healthy up until her pregnancy with me. Thus…I had been blamed for her death, labeled as the culprit behind it.

My father and brother had taken the measures to have me in the care of the best nannies after she had died, though, trying not to hold it against me that my birth had killed the young queen; having me tutored and praised and lavished with luxury but taught to be cool and collected, as expected of a princess of the north...

My brother was a little cold to me, but that was typical of a half-sibling, especially one who had no close ties to the step-mother who had birthed me. From what I had heard, he hadn't been on very friendly terms with her, but had not been opposed to having a sibling...so long as I didn't come for his title.

My father hadn't been a particularly warm person, but he was dutiful and had been sure that I had all that I had needed growing up. He had been a very reserved person.

During a great war with the mages, the nobles had taken it upon themselves to experiment with an ancient power that had been lost away for centuries—the power to absorb the use the drakes.

When a noble child turned ten years of age, they were taken to a special ceremony space to call forth a drake companion that corresponded with their area and powers to match their companions. It was a special privilege that only noble children got to have.

Those companions were for life, and those powers were highly coveted.

When *I* had turned ten, and had failed to produce any powers...

I could still remember the way that my father's face had fallen, and he took me away from the power summit with force; dragging me hard enough that my delicate wrist had been bruised and my arm had been sore for *days*.

A wizard had come from the temple, and had examined me quite thoroughly. He had, in that moment, forever changed the worth of my existence when he took my father to the side of the room.

He told my father that I wasn't simply holding dormant power, but rather...*I was powerless.*

I was a dud.

A *failure*.

Such a thing never occurred in the noble families, and my parentage was immediately questioned.

Had my mother had an affair?

Even if she had, she was still of a noble family herself, so I should have had at least *some* of the powers of a noble as well.

Had she tricked my father?

It was unlikely, as I had inherited his white and silver hair and his gray, stormy eyes. I didn't look like my mother.

My mother had dark grey hair and bright blue eyes, and I bore a striking resemblance to my father.

Once the lack of ability or power had been confirmed by two wizards and a priest, I had been locked away in a shabby, run-down, abandoned warehouse at the edge of the estate, surrounded by snow-covered forest.

My single servant was very bitter to have to watch after *me*, the shame of the family, and she didn't take very good care of me. I was often left to bathe, dress and feed myself, and spent my time in rags and filth like a beast rather than a princess.

My tutoring had stopped, too, and I was left at a ten-year-old's level of education.

At the very least, I had found a beautiful clearing at the edge of the forest, where there grew dozens of what would become my favorite flower. Snapdragons, white ones. Dozens and dozens.

When I had turned eleven, I received the news that my father had passed away.

I learned that my brother had taken up the mantle of his title as the King of the North, and he had taken over my care...though, not that this had really changed anything in regards to me.

I was still the disregarded princess of rags in the warehouse out on the outer edge of the estate.

Within just the last two weeks, however, he suddenly had demanded that the maid start feeding me better meals, and to be sure not to let any marks be found on my body so that I could be married off.

I had questioned the maid, but she had refused to answer any of my questions, insisting that I should feel honored to be of use.

Finally.

At the least, I could bring my family honor through a powerful marriage alliance.

My father—now, my brother, the new king—had a powerful military force and important supplies for the cold that were only produced in our kingdom, and so we were powerful allies to have.

As the new King of the North, it was his duty to strengthen his position and gain powerful allies to be sure that he was a powerful lord.

The snow-wyverns had been acting out a bit lately, as it were, so more kingdoms were dealing with harsher winters, and everyone wanted to create trading deals with my brother anyway.

Our wealth as a nation was growing rapidly.

It was the best time, now, to send me off into a political marriage to unite us for that very benefit.

When I learned that I would be married off, I had sat outside in the snow and cried for some time, staring at the snapdragon flowers that seemed to thrive here ever since I first found them.

I knew that my brother and I weren't close, but for him to send me away so *quickly*...only a year after father had passed away, and still a year before my coming-of-age.

I hadn't even had my social debut—though, I never would have, even if I'd stayed here.

He must desperately wish to be rid of me.

I didn't blame him.

From *his* perspective, his father had remarried so quickly after the death of his own mother, and he had been just adjusting to that new set of circumstances when my mother had died shortly after giving birth to me.

We hadn't ever had much chance to get closer as siblings, as he had spent most of his childhood learning how to be the next King of the North, learning his duties, and I had been learning how to be a proper noble lady.

When I had come to the age-of-power and been proven worthless, I had spent the rest of my days isolated.

The only thing that I would really miss when I left would be my safe haven at the edge of the forest...the flowers, where I had spent much of my time and poured out my woes.

On my last day at the palace, my brother had sent the maids to get me dressed in my wedding attire, bathing me and dressing me and being sure that I looked at least somewhat like a lady of high value.

Nobody would tell me who had been chosen to be my husband, but I didn't feel that it was a good time to press the issue.

I looked back at the castle that had once been my home, but I hadn't been inside the castle in four years.

With one last bow, I looked to my brother, who was sending his personal knight as an envoy to give the marriage agreement papers to the emissaries that would be receiving me on behalf of my husband.

"Do *not* fail me," he said, his tone cold. "This is your only worth to me, so you should be careful be wise with your value."

I bowed lower. "Yes, brother. I will do my best to honor our family."

"My family," he said, cold, and I startled. "*You* are now no more a part of this house. You are marrying into a new family, after all. But you will be a representative of our house, and thus our reputation still rides on your behavior. Don't do anything foolish."

I gave a nod, gulping at the feel of finality.

I would likely never see my brother nor my home again.

I took in his dark, silky gray hair and his bright blue eyes with a dark gray starburst pattern just around the iris, looking like a blizzard.

Then, I turned, and I strained and winced as I pulled myself up into the carriage, looking out and watching as the scenery started moving.

I had hurt my wrists pulling myself inside, and I trembled as I clutched my arms close to my chest.

I wasn't entirely sure *where* I was going, but I did, thankfully, get to know that an envoy was meeting us halfway during the journey, along with an interpreter.

It had to be far, if the actual languages differed.

All of the lords in our area and the water-serpent territory to the east spoke the same language, so it must not be close by.

I knew that I wasn't an important lady to my brother, but I was surprised that he had sent some knights with us. It must be an important marriage to him, for him to care about my safety.

Dressed in this gown of sheer fabric and lace and light material, it was rather cold outside. I was concerned that I may get a cold at this rate.

If I had gained my powers, I would be naturally resistant to the cold, but being powerless, I was just like any of the commoners in the area.

Being of noble blood, meant inheriting powers from the drakes of your region.

In the snow-wyvern territory, the snow-wyverns were resistant to the cold, resistant to poisons, and could create snow storms, ice or light snow with their magic and their breath.

They preferred the cold, and kept it cold in the north.

The nobles of this world had all asked a drake of each class to become humanoid, to mate with them and strengthen the royal bloodlines. This had been possible, only thanks to the sorcerers.

My father's bloodline had chosen the north, for its location and its resistance to poison and cold. Most people couldn't bear to come this far north, and froze to death without special transportation or magics to keep them safe from the bitter cold of our country.

There were the Snow-wyverns and snow-Amphipteres of the North.

Then, there were Earth-drakes and earth-basilisks of the West.

There were Water-sea-serpents and water-leviathans of the East.

Then, the Air-Fae and the Air-Ying-Long of the Central plains.

Lastly, there were the Fire-Dragons and Fire-Griffons of the South, where the imperial city was located.

The Fire-Drake Dynasty had ruled for seven hundred and twenty-four years, now.

Before then, the world had been under the rule of the Earth drake dynasty, who had ruled for almost a thousand years.

The next in line for the earth nation had, however, fallen in love with the next in line for the fire kingdom, and so, the leadership had passed to the fire-drake empire.

I wondered idly where we would be going…

Would I be a prisoner there, too?

Wary caution rose in my gut.

Chapter 2 – Nieves

It had been almost nine hundred years since the continent was reunited.

Once a strong, powerful empire, before being broken into factions: The Mage Faction, and the Knight Faction.

Due to a significantly traumatic event, the factions began a war that lasted one hundred and fifty years.

Upon that anniversary, the king of the Knight's Faction saved the life of a young adept mage noblewoman who was set to marry the next king of a Mage ruled country.

Thus, a new era where the mages and knights tried to reunite and become peaceful began, and despite that it took a couple hundred years, eventually, it became possible.

The Great Queen, Kynareth—a half-blooded mage—as well as her children and her followers, ushered in a time of accepting mages among the nobility of the Knight Faction.

Her son, King Canderoth, along with the help of the other followers, created the Five Kingdoms: The North, South, East, West and Central kingdoms, each run by one of the important members of that group, and King Canderoth became the Emperor over the united kingdoms.

That had been almost nine hundred years ago.

One hundred years passed, and the Paladins gathered, noticing discord among the nobility and other neighboring nations who were getting restless against the growing power of their united empire.

The Paladin Sorcerers devised new magic that would reinvent imagination in our world, and nothing would ever be the same again.

They summoned powerful, long-thought extinct creatures from the world...

The Drakes.

Each kingdom in the empire became a special summoner of two drake types of the same kingdom. For instance, the Northern Kingdom took ownership of the Snow Wyverns and Snow Amphipteres.

The noble families used special magics to sign a contract with the creatures so that only they could summon them in a special coming-of-age tradition...

Now, we were entering into the first month of the seven hundredth and twenty-second year of the rule of the Fire Drake Dynasty...and I was getting married to their tyrant of an emperor.

I was terrified, horrified and likely to die, from how I saw things going.

I wasn't convinced that I would make it through this alive

January, 722 F.D.D. (Fire-Drake Dynasty)

Three weeks had passed, and we were just now coming upon the halfway-marker of the kingdom that I was marrying into.

It had been a long, isolated, unbearably quiet journey, as the guards refused to conversate with me and preferred to spend their time whispering and gossiping about me instead.

I sighed, stretching a bit, but flinching when I felt the pain shoot through my wrist.

I hadn't just strained it getting into the carriage all of this time...now, it was actually damaged. I could hardly hold a spoon for soup, at this point, let alone anything else.

The knights cared nothing of my struggles, however; they were simply charged with getting me safely to my meeting place with the envoy from the kingdom I was marrying into.

I heard a horn blow, and I startled in my seat in the carriage, looking out of the window and seeing a group of wagons and a single carriage approaching us.

We met off to the side of the path, and my knights waited for me to get out.

I slid out of the carriage gingerly, stretching and trying to ignore the stiffness of my joints before I used my arms to lift my two suit-cases into my arms, and the knights who stood in red and gold uniforms startled, before two rushed over to take my bags from me when they noticed that my knights weren't lifting a single finger to assist me.

I heard the knights of my betrothed's kingdom muttering and whispering in a language that I didn't understand, and I glanced at them warily.

I was shocked, however, to see that nobody looked at me with unfriendly eyes…though, to be fair, I was still wearing and veil and they couldn't see my face. I was covered from head to toe.

It had been a good thing, too, because before I had left, I had been struck by a maid for asking her where I was going.

She had struck me in the face, telling me that it wasn't my place to question those things.

I sighed softly, glancing around.

"Princess! My lady, princess Nieves of the North, it is good to meet you. I am your interpreter, Kerik Blaze. We humbly welcome you and thank you for your effort on this long journey," he said, and he gave me a formal bow.

I gaped as the rest of the knights did the same, and I looked behind me with tears stinging my eyes when my knights snickered at their show of respect for me.

I knew that my people thought I was worthless…

My interpreter glanced behind me, and glared at them. "Did I speak something funny? Did I misinterpret? Is my accent funny?"

They glanced away, ignoring him.

"You should take more care, for I would hate to have to alert my emperor to any maltreatment of his new bride."

I almost choked on the air I was breathing. "P-pardon?" I asked, startled.

Emperor...?

He glanced at me; surprise evident on his face. "My lady?" He asked.

"Who...*who* did you say I am I marrying?"

He looked at me with confusion. "...Have you not been informed, princess?" He asked, surprised. "You have been married to the emperor, my lady. Emperor Kai Abeloth."

My heart dropped in the pit of my stomach.

Could this news have been any worse? I may has well have been sentenced to death.

How could this have been my fate?

What had I done so wrong? Was I being punished for being a failure?

Seeing who my brother was, the cold-blooded demon, he must be punishing me, surely.

I would probably be dead by the next month...

Kai Abeloth was the world's most notorious, tyrannical, sadistic, war-mongering death-reaper with a temper that could set a person on fire with a single look.

That...that *monster*...was my husband...?

I felt faint.

The knights behind me snickered again, and my interpreter shot them a menacing glare.

He wasn't a particularly *big* man, but his fiery gaze was intimidating.

"What in the world is *so damn funny*?" He asked, exasperated.

"You may not realize it, but that girl..." they cracked up, laughing too hard to even finish their thought.

I glanced to the interpreter.

"I am so sorry, lord Blaze," I said, giving a curtsy. "I hope you are not offended. I am so embarrassed to meet you with such disrespectful knights from my kingdom."

He waved it off, gesturing to my carriage. "Let us finish getting your things, then, and then we—"

"Pardon me, but...I have nothing else," I said, and he gaped at me.

"What?" He asked, stunned. "Surely, you have more. What princess travels with so few possessions?"

"Well..." I looked away, tugging the hem of my veil and wringing it in my hands.

"We brought six wagons to be sure that we had enough room for your things, my lady," he said, stunned. "But to think you only had two small bags?" He glanced to the knights, and told them quickly the updates situation.

They all gaped and gasped, looking at one another in surprise and looking at me as if I were some pitiful, sorrowful soul.

Perhaps I was.

"But...am I really getting married to that...that scary man?" I practically squeaked, and he smiled warmly at me.

"Oh, not to worry, my lady. The emperor will not harm you...so long as you do not harm him, nor his treasures."

"Oh, I see," I said, though...I didn't quite feel reassured.

We gave a quick farewell to the knights after they presented the dowry to the interpreter, who loaded the chests of jewels and mana stones into two of the wagons.

Two wagons' worth of jewels and priceless mana stones, plants, herbs, winter supplies and medicines and poisons specially made in the north, in exchange for taking me off his hands and out of his hair.

A small price to pay, indeed, for my brother.

A small price to be rid of the shame of my name on his family registry, the stain on his bloodline.

I felt tears prickle my eyes as I watched the knights from my homeland disappear.

It was official. I was going.

Not that I'd been given a choice.

As a useless lady, this was my only possible purpose to begin with.

I could only hope that my interpreter was right; that I wouldn't be harmed.

I walked to the new carriage that I would be riding in, and when I went to get up into it on my own, the knights around us gawked at me in shock and two of them rushed over to help me, sputtering out in a language that sounded like gibberish to me.

I glanced to my interpreter, and he cleared his throat, looking away. "They are appalled that a princess would be entering a carriage without assistance that way, so they wish to help you. They feel guilty for not knowing that you were ready to enter."

I smiled. "It is alright. I've been getting in and out of the carriage on my own during the entirety of my journey," I said, wincing when one of the knights took my hand to help me step up.

He gaped, startled at my show of pain, glancing back at the interpreter and telling him something.

"You mean...nobody has been assisting you? Is...is that why you are injured?" My interpreter asked.

I glanced to my swollen hand and wrist, in the tender grasp of a knight who watched me with wide, pitying eyes.

I looked back to my interpreter, giving a nod, and the interpreter translated the situation.

"I had heard that the Northerners were cold-blooded, but you are their princess. You are of a very high-lineage. How could they treat you in such a way?"

The group of knights whispered, and I sighed, huffing and pulling my wrist from the knight with a groan, stepping up into the carriage on my own even as the knights tried to stop me.

"Mister interpreter, I am not in need of coddling. I can get by on my own. Rather, this show of kindness is making me uncomfortable. I would rather you treat me as my own knights do; treat me as if I am scum, a disservice to the north, as that is what I am accustomed to."

He scratched the back of his head, before he translated what I said for the knights.

They all looked around, somewhat wary and not really agreeable, but they closed the carriage door and the envoy began on our way again, my carriage in the middle of the caravan.

As we continued our journey south, the temperature continued to get warmer as we got further away from the north.

I was getting sweaty and uncomfortable, wishing to at least bathe.

Though…was I allowed to change clothes?

I had been subjected to wearing my wedding attire during the whole of the trip thus far. Would they get angry if I wanted to stop to rest?

If I asked to bathe…?

The first few days that we had travelled, my interpreter had been rather shocked to see me reject eating more than one meal a day, and that I only drank one glass of water each day.

The other knights regularly glanced at my carriage, whispering with my interpreter with concerned expressions on their faces.

I wasn't sure what he was telling them or what their opinions were, but it wasn't my concern.

I wasn't important, after all.

I wasn't comfortable with kindness when I knew, deep down, that they would forsake me the moment they found out the truth about me.

I didn't have the powers of the north.

I couldn't create snow. I couldn't freeze things. I wasn't resistant to the cold, nor to poisons.

Not only that...but I couldn't ride the wyverns. I didn't even have one of my own, as a noble was supposed to.

The greatest power that the noble families of the elements had, was the ability to summon and ride the respective drake-types of their nations.

When a noble boy or girl came to the age of power at ten years old, they would summon a drake that was born on the same day as them, to form their destined bond and create a contract of power.

When we had gone to the summit and I had undergone the ceremony...only for none of the north's powers to manifest, nor any young wyvern to appear to form our bond...

It was the greatest sign of shame. It had never happened in the history of the royal families.

I had been a dud. Useless.

Worthless.

I trembled at the thought of my new husband finding out the truth, and what he would think.

Would he kill me for having the insolence to come all this way and be his bride when I had no power?

I had nothing to offer him.

I hadn't even bled yet, so I couldn't have children.

I hadn't been taught the responsibilities of a wife or the management of a household nor a kingdom. As soon as the reality of my worth had come to light, I had been cast away and my lessons as a noble lady had stopped altogether.

The only reason that I knew about the monthly cycles and their purpose was because that was taught at a young age, as it could start at an early age.

We came to a stop, and I began to panic as I glanced out of the window of the carriage.

I saw that we had come to a great river, with a bridge to cross, and only one carriage was crossing at a time.

"Princess, we will be moving again momentarily. This bridge is older, so we only cross one vehicle at a time for safety precautions."

"I see. That isn't a problem." I took a deep whiff, and I smelled salt in the air. "What is that smell from?"

"Ah, right," he said. "You are from the north, and have likely never smelled the ocean before. The Southern kingdom is located on the Southern borders, and just beyond the mountains that edge our kingdom is the ocean."

"Oh, I see," I said.

"By the way, princess, when can we be expecting your drake to come to the south?" He asked.

I startled. "W-what?"

"Well surely, we didn't expect for you two to be parted. That is a crucial bond, of course. Do you have a wyvern? Or the other drake type of the northern region?"

"Oh...I, um..." I tried to think of an excuse. "I didn't want for it to come South. It is so hot here; it would probably be uncomfortable."

He looked at me as if I were saying something completely strange...but thankfully, he didn't press me any further.

I sighed when we started moving again, taking my mind back to the movement of the carriage and off of the plaguing question.

Would he shame me when he found out the truth?

Would Kai be angry for being gifted a worthless doll?

All that I had was my looks, after all.

I had heard the knights in the north, many times, talking about what a shame it was that I was so beautiful and yet had no value beyond my appearance.

I wasn't even *worthy* to breed.

I felt my stomach rumbling painfully, clenching with my discomfort.

I would probably be dead soon enough. I was positive.

We got over the bridge and continued onward for a few more hours, before I heard a great noise.

I glanced out of the carriage window again, and saw the swarming of people as we began to pass through a city. They were cheering and were wearing happy, excited faces.

They were…*welcoming me…?*

I had never been welcomed in such a way since I was ten. It felt nice, but I quickly tried to push down the greedy feeling of wanting to keep receiving this love.

I knew that it wouldn't last long…

I sighed painfully, shutting the curtains, and I could feel the energy shifting as I disappeared from their view.

"Princess…?" My interpreter asked, concerned confusion on his face.

He didn't understand, *yet*, but he would soon enough.

"I haven't ever been fond of crowds," I said, my voice shaky. "I get nervous around people."

"Oh," he said. "I suppose, seeing that your father died and you've been married before you made your debut in society, you likely haven't had the opportunity to be around many people."

I didn't respond to that, and he didn't press me for more conversation.

We pulled up to a stop, and he stretched, stepping out of the carriage and lifting his hand in offering to me.

I took it hesitantly, letting him help me down.

The act would begin now…because, for my own safety, I couldn't let this emperor find out that I was a fraudulent sack of worthlessness.

I couldn't let him discover that his bride was not the noble, powerful wintry princess he had signed for, bought with a massive engagement gift sent to my homeland, and had brought all the way here with an entourage of knights to escort me safely.

Those things costed money, effort and work. If he found out that it was all for a worthless girl like me, I could only imagine how disappointed he would be…maybe enough to kill me.

More than anything, I couldn't let down my brother and our house, who were depending on me to play the part of the empress and make this warlord happy so that they could further their own political position.

It was the one and only thing that I could do to better my house, and the only purpose I served.

I had to be sure I pleased this emperor.

I could do it.

If I *couldn't*, my brother wouldn't have entrusted me with such an important task…right?

I tried to hold out hope for that, at least. He probably hoped that I would die quickly, without bringing shame to him in any way, but I hoped that he actually loved and cared for me and trusted me.

It was a silly notion, to be sure, but it comforted me if but for an instant.

A butler came out of the palace and down the stairs, bowing to welcome us.

He spoke to us in his mother tongue, and the interpreter translated.

"The butler, Markus, says, 'Welcome, Princess of the North. We are honored to have you here, and to have you become our empress. It was a careful selection for our emperor, and you are very wanted and welcomed here. We will do our best to make you feel at home. Our emperor is currently crushing an uprising that rose a few hours away, but he should be back shortly.' I will be accompanying you as the butler leads you on a tour."

We stepped into the palace, and I was dazzled by the bright reds and oranges and golds that decorated the enormous space of this palace, the suits of armor the knights wore…

It was brilliant. So much more colorful and dazzling than the cool grays, whites and blues of the North.

We walked through to a large glass door, opening up to a brilliant courtyard and garden with magnificent fountains and beautiful foliage all around.

There was a landing pad that was brought to my attention as, at that very moment, we heard the call of a dragon.

I looked up to the skies to see the blazing fire shooting into the air in a sign of victory, even as a rider pumped up his sword in triumph.

The knights of the palace shouted as they all congregated to the landing pad, and I watched in awed-horror as the rider descended on the great dragon with red and golden scales with a back-setting of black scales for the majority.

He shimmered and shined brilliantly. Black horns protruded from his head, and his dazzling golden eyes blinked as he noticed me.

He roared out something almost like speech, and I heard the rider respond to him in kind, before they finally landed, shaking the ground with the thunderous weight hitting the ground.

The rider dismounted with unexpected grace for a large man, and as he approached me, I noticed that he was splattered with blood.

He was dressed in brilliant black armor, with a red cape that was emboldened by golden embroidery in the shape of his crest, and his helmet was topped with a shot of red and gold feathering, fraying fur, it looked like.

He removed his helmet and tucked it beneath his left arm, shoving his bloody black-bladed sword into the earth between us, and he gave a slight bow.

He lifted his hand up in offering, and I took it, feeling the heat radiating through his hands even through the metal of his armor.

I took in his brilliant, flaming orange-red hair with lowlights of auburn and highlights of gold. He had bright, sparkling burnt-orange eyes. He had dark, rich tan skin, and a dashing, pearly-white smile.

He was stunning.

If this man was anyone *but* the emperor, I would have been utterly stunned by the power he exuded considering that he wasn't.

He had to be my husband. There was simply no one else in this vicinity who radiated this much royal power.

He uttered something in his rich, smooth, buttery voice, and the interpreter turned to me.

"Emperor Kai says, 'Welcome, my bride, to your new home. I have won a great victory over a rebellion in your honor to welcome you.'"

I gasped with the realization that I had been right; this really was my husband.

I came back to my senses, turning to him, and I smiled demurely before I gave a deep, perfected curtsy.

I just hoped I wasn't too out of practice for him to take notice of it.

"I am honored to be here, your majesty," I said.

He perked up at my voice, seemingly pleased, and glanced to my interpreter, who told him what I had said.

The emperor said something again, before I looked to my translator.

"He says, 'We shall adjourn for the evening after a good meal. You will stay in guest chambers until the coronation tomorrow.'"

I glanced to my translator. "Coronation…?"

"You will be coronated as empress tomorrow, and from that point forward, you will stay in the emperor and empress's chambers. It is a room that is adjoined together, with a door in between the two, but allows for immediate access to one another at any time. I am sure you can guess why."

My heart rate picked up as he and the emperor conversed for a moment.

"Dinner will be served in your room, for tonight. There will be a grand banquet in honor of your coronation and welcoming for you tomorrow."

I curtsied again. "I see. Very well. Please show me to my quarters," I said to the translator, and he acquiesced to my request.

Chapter 3 - Kai Abeloth

November, 721 Fire Drake Dynasty

"You *have* to pick a groom for the princess, your majesty!" My counselor said, determined. "You have said that you refuse to remarry, but the princess cannot inherit the throne. Your previous empress passed away of sickness years ago, and the princess needs a mother, but you refuse. Our kingdom needs an heir, whether that be by you or the princess... *Our kingdom* needs an heir, a *male* heir! There are many eligible lords for the princess, or ladies for you available...Lady Blaze—"

I slammed my hand on the table, my eyes stinging as my head throbbed. "I didn't even want the empress that I had!" I shouted. "You lot married her off to me and then waited until I was deep in sleep to—" I cut myself off, groaning. "Now you want to force that same scenario on my daughter? No. My daughter can be the heir, for all I care. What does she or I need to get married for?" I snarled.

"You are about to be twenty-one, your majesty. The princess will be coming of marriageable age soon enough. You need a male heir, as the emperor. It is your duty to carry on the bloodlines. We can arrange a marriage for you again, and if you wish to wait, you can, but—"

"*Fine*," I said, firm. "I will marry. I will not have you push my daughter into an arranged marriage, and force her to become a brood mare just to pump out heirs for the kingdom. I will...force myself to push past my grievances and remarry. However, I have some conditions."

"Great, your majesty! Please, tell me."

"I want someone who is too young to give me heirs right away. Last time you married me off, you gave me a bride older than me, and she mounted me like a breeding horse in my sleep! I do not want such a thing again. I want a younger bride, who can *grow with me*...rather than us being forced to bed under obligation and 'duty'."

The advisors murmured, disconcerted, but the main advisor waved it off. "*Fine*. Anything else?"

I considered that. "I do not wish for her to be of this kingdom."

They all gaped at me. "*What?*"

"I will not marry another Fire-Drake bred woman. Bring me someone completely different. I want someone who will be a drastic contrast to the former empress."

They all glanced at one another, concerned.

This was, after all, an unparalleled, abnormal request.

No emperor of the Fire Drake Dynasty had wed outside of the Fire-Drake lands in over three hundred years...for good reason.

The last emperor who *had*, had been plotted against and killed by his Wind empress.

She had been caught and convicted, expelled through death, but the crown had fallen to the prince next in line and we hadn't married outside of our own noble families in that time since.

"Your majesty, please, reconsid—"

"*I refuse*," I told him. "You either pass succession rights to the princess, or you bring in a younger girl from another land. That is the only two options I will agree to."

"Your majesty," the wizard spoke up, showing us a map on the wall. "I know of a kingdom that is quite powerful, and they have a princess who is *just under* marrying age…however, her brother just became the king there, as their father died last year. He is already seeking other arrangements for her. Many outside nations have expressed interest in her."

"Hm," I said. "You are referring to the Northern kingdom, aren't you?"

"That is correct, your majesty," he said, his red eyes twinkling. "With the young king now in charge, he will be looking to strengthen himself with powerful allies. What better ally to have than the emperor of the imperial city himself?"

"How old is he?" I asked. "To become the king through the death of his father."

"The same age you were when your father died at war, I believe," an advisor spoke up. "Zabbix is right, your majesty. This king of the north will be looking to gain powerful friends. And, the Northern families are quite powerful and will offer a calm, cool, collected bride for you. From what I have always seen, the women of the north are always good looking, as well."

I glanced to the butler. "Prepare a letter asking for marriage, right away," I said, and he scurried off to do my bidding.

A girl of the North, hm…?

The documents sent, the answer had arrived; The papers were signed, and the dowry agreed upon.

Yes.

The king of the North, the ambitious and desperate young king that he was, *was in fact looking to make powerful allies.*

In exchange for the marriage to his younger sister, I would be receiving much-needed winter supplies, herbs, poison recipes, antidote recipes, winter clothing models for the south, and a sizeable dowry of gold, gems and mana stones.

In return, I would be sending two battalions' worth of army forces, a bunch of supplies from our own kingdom, livestock to help supply to their farmers, grains, plants that only grew in the south, produce, and steel for weapons.

I quickly arranged for an interpreter for the girl, whom I learned was aged twelve and was named Nieves Eirwen, which literally translated in their mother tongue to "*Maiden of the Blessed Snow.*"

I glanced to a portrait of the former empress, and I scowled.

I had been angry for quite some time because of her. I had been confused and angered, filled with conflicting emotion.

Only one good thing had come from my union with that woman;

My princess...my daughter...was already eight years of age, so anyone could do the math.

I had been thirteen when I had become a father.

Thinking of the empress brought on a flurry of mixed emotion.

I remembered it still; dining with my empress, who was beautiful in her own right.

She had been recently married to me, me at the age of twelve and she at the age of nineteen.

I had recently taken the throne, and the people were desperate to secure the lineage of succession as I was already actively involved in war.

So, when I wasn't aware, the council were working with the empress to secure a means to ensure that I would create said heir.

We had dined that night as we normally would, and I had found it a bit odd that my empress had watched me with a strange light in her eyes as she pushed me to not only drink some wine, but to down an entire glass. It was too late to realize what had happened when, later that night, I was waking up from a deep, drug-induced slumber and thinking that I was in a dream...until I had realized that I was tied down to my bed, and I panicked and cried as my nineteen-year-old empress thrust herself on top of me wildly, crying out with abandon with her head back and a sickeningly pleased look upon her face.

"I am the empress, the most powerful woman of this empire," she whined. "I will give the emperor his heir!"

She seemed particularly inebriated herself, repeating this phrase like a chant to justify her actions.

I remembered the feeling of her insides, how they tightened as I found my body forced into submission…how my body unwillingly reached its physical peak, and tears ran down my face as I experienced my very first release.

It had been stolen from me.

Only weeks later, she was confirmed to be pregnant.

I would later learn that she had taken a drug to enhance fertilization, as well, so that her chances of insemination were far higher than usual.

One time was all it took, and I thanked the heavens for that, in itself.

After the pregnancy and the birth of our daughter—whom she despised, because she hadn't birthed a male heir for me—she had attempted to force herself on me again.

I caught her and threatened to kill her if she did it again, so she started manipulating me and working over me with her charms. She tried to win my love through affection and attention, pining away over me even as she ignored our child.

I had been very confused by my feelings; she had been the one and only woman I had been intimate with, and that had formed an attachment that I couldn't explain.

As I blossomed into a man, I wanted to be inside of her again, to feel her around me again. It had been a feeling I had enjoyed, despite the perverseness of her actions in that moment.

Her sweet affections for me and her attention made me almost...love her, too.

She doted on me, and I was too young to realize that all she wanted was the fame and glory of a rightful empress.

However, when I was fifteen, I found her in my bed again, drunk and high on aphrodisiacs, begging me to breed her like a race horse again and let her bare a son for me, begging me to give her seed.

I had felt my skin crawl as she tried to climb atop of me without my consent once more, begging to be bred again.

I finally realized, in that moment, that all she had ever wanted from me was to breed me and provide the next emperor.

As the emperor's mother, she held special benefits and luxuries that even the empress was denied.

The Dowager Empress was the highest authority because she had the ability to oppose an emperor unless the entire council outvoted her.

Essentially, if I made an order and my mother didn't agree, she could override my order unless the entire council also agreed with my order.

My empress wanted that authority for herself, to give me a son whom she could run the scenes behind.

Once I realized this, well...it was all a matter of taking the situation into my own control.

I couldn't allow this woman to become an even stronger power in my empire. As the emperor, a fifteen-year-old young man who, even as a thirteen-year-old boy had already been fighting in wars, I had to protect my people. If I didn't, then who else would?

I began to put a few drops of poison in her tea every tea time and meal time.

She slowly grew to be sick, and within two more years and by the time that I had turned seventeen, she was dead.

I sighed, looking away from the portrait of the empress to a better, grander portrait of the only girl who *currently* resided in my heart; my daughter.

Princess Conlaed Fiammetta Abeloth.

She had gotten my fiery hair, but her mother's bright golden eyes, as well as my rich tan skin.

She was a beautiful girl, and if I was honest, I did feel guilty that she didn't have a mother.

Her mother had hated her, and had refused to even see her once she had been born and deemed female.

I tried, with all of my might, to give the girl all of the tender love and warmth that I could possibly give, blazing through her heart and mind with the heat of my passionate fatherly care for her.

I may have hated how she had come to be, but I loved her, and that was enough. She was my princess.

I idly wondered how my new bride would get along with my daughter, who I would admit was rather spoiled and pampered. She was my greatest treasure, after all. She, and my dragon, Flame, were my closest treasures.

Upon receiving the confirmation of acceptance for my new bride, I had also received a portrait of her.

She had soft, silky silver hair and dark, stormy grey eyes with the faintest hint of blue.

She looked like winter.

She had pale, pale skin and looked rather small, but that was to be expected, I supposed.

I looked forward to meeting her, at least. This would be the first bride of my own choosing, and I had done quite a bit of research about the north when I had made my choice.

I had learned a great deal about their customs and way of life, and I hoped that was enough to impress her.

I didn't intend to have a sexual relationship with her for quite some time.

I was nine years older than she was, so it almost felt *too big* of an age gap, but there had been many noble ladies wed to men much older and much younger with bigger gaps, so I tried not to stress about that too much.

Nieves...

I would be meeting her in a few short weeks.

It was three weeks later that I had received the news that there was an uprising in a nearby city, and I very casually, nonchalantly took my dragon there and laid waste to their armies rather quickly.

It had taken all of about a month to find and destroy all of their forces, my dragon fighting from the air even as I clashed swords with the vagrants below.

It was easy and over quickly. Not even a challenge.

On a quick fly over on the way home, I saw the caravan arriving at the palace; I was happy to be arriving back at the same time that my bride was arriving herself.

I had been anticipating this moment, and to bring home a victory over such filth at the same time?

It was good omen, indeed.

I landed Flame on the landing space near the courtyard, striding to her in a confident fashion, when I noticed the minute trembling of her body.

She was even smaller than I had anticipated.

I knew that I was older than her, but she seemed unnaturally small, even for her age.

My eight-year-old daughter wasn't much smaller than she was.

She was a princess, wasn't she...?

Shouldn't she be...*average*, at **least**?

Even over weight was what I would have expected.

Although, I realized that things were barren in the north. Perhaps she was *very* well-fed, for a princess of the north...?

She wasn't what I had anticipated, certainly...though, I noted with pleasure, that she was even more lovely and far prettier than even her portrait had made her out to be. Her stormy, blizzard-night eyes came to life as light reflected off of them and I could see the life in her.

I could see, however, that even though she put on a brave face, there was deep-rooted fear in her gaze.

Was she...afraid of *me*?

When I heard her speak, I decided quickly that I liked the cool, tinkling sound of her small voice.

She was reserved, though I noted that her legs strained with the effort of her curtsies.

She looked to be forcing the balance, over compensating for being out of practice.

Being such a sharp man who had been brought up in war and battle, she couldn't hide these things from me.

<u>I was used to intimidating others, after all.</u>

I had sent her on her way, and once the interpreter returned from taking her to her arranged chambers, I pulled him to the side.

"Tell me everything," I said. "She isn't as I had anticipated."

"Her knights were *very* rude to her from the start, your majesty. They were...quite mocking and degrading toward her. She even admitted that she had been underfed and under-cared-for the entire trip."

"What?" I snarled.

"She had even been getting in and out of the carriage without assistance."

"But...but she is a *princess*," I said, baffled. "I read all about her bloodline. Her mother was the daughter of a duke of the north, and her father was the king of the north. She has two *impeccable* bloodlines. She even looks greatly like her brother and the former king...I don't understand."

He shook his head. "I also thought it strange that she refused help the rest of the time we were on our journey, and insisted we not be exceedingly kind to her. When checked on, she had already taken care of her base needs before the maid with us could even get to her. It seemed rather instinctual for her to care for herself on her own."

I considered this. "Anything else?"

He glanced away, before he looked back to me. "She brought only two small bags of belongings with her."

"What?" I gaped, surprised even as the knights were bringing in those very bags to her chambers as we spoke. "I am so confused," I said.

"She also...cries in her sleep, your majesty. She has seemed blatantly terrified and anxious the entire journey here."

"That is not the behavior of a beloved, cherished blooming lady," I said, contemplating all of this. "What on earth is going on here?"

"The knights were picking fun at her, saying we didn't even know, something...but they just laughed and went on their way without an explanation."

I looked after where my bride had gone. "Something is rather odd, here."

"Yes, your majesty."

"Continue spending time around her, and report back to me with any new developments."

"Yes, sire."

This wasn't right...this wasn't right at all.

I needed to figure out what was really going on, here.

Chapter 4 – Kai

The following morning arrived, and I rushed to get dressed in one of my finest uniforms.

I was getting formally married today.

Though the paperwork was already signed, we were holding the official ceremony at her coronation as empress, and then we would hold a huge feast in her honor.

There was only one thing about the day that I was not looking forward to.

I cringed when I imagined how my daughter would react to her new step-mother.

I remembered how she had reacted when one of my advisors had asked me to dance with his daughter for her social debut…

A dance. That was it.

My daughter had thrown a *fit*—more like a meltdown—insisting that I could only dance with her, that I could only have her as the one lady of my life.

I laughed as I thought about it, though.

My daughter was so selfish with me. A tyrant in her own right.

She would have to get over that, though, and *quickly*.

Of course, if the new empress bullied or hurt my daughter in any way, I was adequately prepared to dispose of her, fucking immediately.

I knew, though, that I couldn't be rash. My daughter was spoiled, and did not like to share me.

I honestly expected some rebellion.

"Everything is ready, sire," my butler said from my doorway. I turned to face him and he smiled, coming and straightening a wrinkle out of my jacket. "There, you look perfect, your majesty."

"Is my bride ready?" I asked, and he nodded.

"Yes, your majesty. She is prepared and dressed. The princess is asking a lot of questions, but I didn't tell her anything, just as you instructed."

"Good," I said with a nod. "I wanted to leave that be as long as I could. You know well how the princess will respond to the news."

"Yes, sire," he said with an amused chuckle. "She will be very upset."

I chuckled under my breath even as we strode through the halls.

"Did my bride eat anything last night?"

"She ate only about a *fifth* of the tray, your majesty. The interpreter says that she ate similar amounts of food during the trip, and that she always left meals rather untouched despite being offered and encouraged to participate in large meals."

"Hm," I said. "Perhaps she has a particular food preference? I realize that there is a drastic difference between the Northern and

Southern cuisine. Perhaps it is to be expected. Still, though, I need to find something that she can eat well, and quickly. I can't have her starving. In any case, we will figure it out and make the necessary adjustments."

"Yes, your majesty. Also, I consulted with the interpreter about the area we prepared for her drake, but—"

"—*But?*" I asked, stopping. "What about it? Is there a problem?"

"She..." He hesitated. "She wasn't *accompanied* by one."

"...*What?*" I asked, baffled. "Any noble lady would bring her companion with her. Hold on, hold on..." I rubbed my temples. "Barely eating, doing everything from bathing to mounting carriages without even waiting for assistance, having very few belongings for such a long journey, very thin and seemingly stunted growth, now she isn't even accompanied by her drake companion?" I crossed my arms. "Something is off. You planted the spy last month like I asked, didn't you?"

"Oh, yes, sire."

"Contact our inside source. I want to get more in-depth information about this girl, as quickly as possible. I am starting to wonder if she is even a noble. Did they send me a maid who looks like my bride, and simply hide away the real princess? That is the only *logical* explanation."

"I will look into it," he said.

"Send word right away."

"Right away, your majesty." He scurried off, even as I continued toward the throne room.

"Announcing the arrival of his majesty, Emperor Kai Abeloth."

I stepped into the room with authority, and I heard the crowd murmuring and making appreciative sounds of my appearance as I strode to the throne, where a priest stood, waiting with a crown in his hand.

I turned toward the doors, waiting.

"Announcing the arrival of her highness, princess Nieves Eirwen," the announcer called, and I smiled as she entered.

She timidly—reminding me of a little snow-rabbit about to be snatched up by a big bad wolf—strode up the aisle with a young girl holding her gown's long train in hand, and she was a vision in silver and white amongst a sea of red and gold.

I noted, with a little disgruntlement, that I could see her chest bones beneath the sheer material covering her upper chest and collarbone.

The bones were peeking through.

She was so unbearably thin...my eight-year-old was thicker.

She reached me, and took my hand shyly as I gave a slight bow, helping her step up the stairs to the throne, and she curtsied deeply before the priest who held the crown.

The interpreter stood there, ready to translate.

I could practically hear her bones creaking from the effort to hold her curtsy...

I turned to her, removing her small tiara, and placed it in the hands of a maid who held a waiting pillow.

"Do you, princess Nieves, vow to honor your duties as the empress? Do you swear to honor your home of the south, and respect the traditions and lives of your subjects? To use your authority with honor and grace, and to have mercy and proper justice in dealing with those subjects? Do you vow to respect me, as emperor, and stand at my side as the ruler of this empire?"

The interpreter quickly translated what I said to her, his voice speaking over her tongue with a refined, dignified manner.

Her language was very smooth and collected, compared to the fast and harsh sound of our language.

She bowed her head, before lifting her gaze to meet mine. "I solemnly swear so to do," she answered as translated, her voice a little shaky but her eyes resolved. The interpreter smiled at me.

I turned us to the priest.

"By the authority given by the Empire of the South, in front of the heavens and in front of the empire, I bless this union and deem you empress." The priest waited for the translator to tell the empress this. Then, he lifted the crown high into the air, before setting it down onto her head. "Long live the emperor! Long live the empress! Long live the empire!"

The throne room roared with applause and chanting that same phrase, cheering for us.

The interpreter whispered what they were saying in her own tongue, and she smiled.

I took her hand, leading her out of the throne room and through the halls to the banquet hall, where a fantastic feast was waiting.

I sat her next to my place, and then sat at the head of the table.

The interpreter sat next to her on her other side, ready to translate.

A servant brought her a plate piled high, and she gazed at the plate as if it were the most mountainous thing she had ever seen.

I smiled. She looked overwhelmed.

"So, is everything to your liking?" I asked, and the interpreter asked her for me.

She startled, looking at her plate before speaking in her tinkling voice, and the interpreter told me what she said.

"She said, 'oh, yes, your majesty. I am just unused to having so much to eat. A lady's virtue is eating lightly and with dignity'..." He said softly, and it seemed as if the phrase was just a repetition she was used to hearing.

"They must not have a lot food in the north," I chuckled.

He translated what I said.

She cringed a little, but took a tentative bite of her food without responding to my statement.

Her eyes lit up and sparkled, but she restrained herself and ate slowly and quietly.

I see, I thought. She wants to eat more, but she is used to strict restrictions. She must feel very pressured. I read that the north was very strict about rules and manners.

"You may eat to your heart's content without reservation," I said, taking my wine and sipping it. "I am rather unconcerned about your manners. You will see that the south isn't as stuffy about decorum as the north, and I am not a husband who demands perfection. Rather, just do your duties and keep yourself occupied, and I will be content."

Though I didn't feel as numb toward her as I had originally anticipated that I would be, I wasn't particularly drawn to interact with her, either. Still, though, I intended to be kind and courteous. She was just a little girl, brought here against her wishes. I knew better than to think she had volunteered to be here.

Honestly, if she followed her duties and didn't bother me, I was sure I would grow affectionate toward her in time.

I didn't want a bride like my last, who would fawn all over me and force herself into my bed against my will.

The translator smiled brightly and told her what I said. She smiled.

"I want you to understand something else, as well. I am not asking for a close, intimate relationship with you…at least, not anytime soon. To be honest, if you do your duties and stay out of my way, I will be courteous and kind to you and be busy with my own duties. I wish to not have my life disturbed."

The translator told her this, also.

This seemed to take some of the tension out of her shoulders, and she ate slightly bigger bites and wasn't waiting so long between bites to take another.

I grinned internally as I watched her enjoy her food, before she winced after taking another bite.

She whispered to the interpreter, suddenly, and he looked surprised before he turned to me.

"Pardon me, your majesty...but she...she says that she has finished," he said, glancing at her plate with a worried expression.

I glanced at her, and she peeked at me, looking up at me from beneath impossibly-thick eyelashes.

I gaped at her plate, gawking at the large amount.

"Are you sure? I will not be offended if you want to eat more. I would enjoy watching you eat several plates. Have as much as you want. Take it to your chambers. I will not be bothered."

The interpreter answered for her once she told him. "'I am full, your majesty, but I appreciate your generosity'."

"*Full?*" I asked, surprised. "But you have eaten only a fraction of a meal for a girl your size. Are you sure?"

Without the interpreter's help, she seemed to understand what I was asking. She glanced to me.

She nodded. "Yes. I am fine," she said in my own tongue, looking down and twiddling her fingers.

I startled, realizing something in that instant.

I realized that not only had I not made any effort to learn any of her language, but now I had criticized her unintentionally.

Uh-oh, I thought. *I made her uncomfortable. I made her nervous.*

I didn't know why, but I suddenly wanted to make sure she was comfortable.

With her small size, she made me think of her almost the way that I thought of a little sister.

I wanted to protect her.

This young girl was now in my care.

As her husband and guardian, I was now officially responsible for her, her care, her protection...I was responsible for it all.

As long as she didn't cross any of my boundaries or get in my way, I would be a dutiful husband by her and protect her well.

She had really lucked up my becoming *my* empress; she had a husband who wouldn't force her to be bedded, and I wouldn't disturb her if she didn't bother me, but I also wouldn't be mean to her.

I would keep her safe, while asking for almost nothing in return.

"Alright, then," I smiled. "If you are sure that you have had your fill, I would be happy to give you a full tour of the palace and we can get to know one another."

The interpreter told her what I said, but I knew that I needed to make more of an effort to learn how to communicate with her without his help.

She had already learned how to say "yes" in my language, which meant that she was trying to communicate on her own, and I needed to reciprocate her efforts.

We were married now, so I needed to accommodate her.

She smiled, and I stood, pulling out her chair and taking her hand.

"There are several dignitaries we need to meet first," I told her through the translator, and led her to a table where all of my advisors were seated.

"It is an honor you meet you, your majesty," my head advisor said, letting the translator convey this to her. "Welcome to the Fire-Drake kingdom. I hope you will enjoy your stay."

"She says, 'thank you for your warm welcome. It will be an adjustment, but it is nice and warm here.'"

"Just wait until the summer," he laughed. "This is quite cool for us."

The interpreter told her what he said.

I glanced to her, introducing her to more people, and a couple of knights who would be her escorts from now on, before we stepped out of the banquet hall.

"I do have someone...rather important that I wish you to meet," I said, smiling at her as the translator told her what I said. "As you know, I am recently turned twenty-one," I said, letting the interpreter tell her, and she nodded. "I...I have to confess to you that you aren't my first wife."

She looked shocked when the interpreter conveyed this.

"She says, 'am I a *queen*, or an *empress*?'"

I chuckled.

It was a valid question, I supposed.

An *empress* was the one with the most power next to the emperor, but often times, emperors took more than one wife.

His most preferred and *proper* wife would be the empress, but other wives became his queens.

"You are the *empress*, and worry not—I do not intend to have any queens."

She was visibly relieved by this when the interpreter told her, and I chuckled as I led her through the halls.

"No, the first empress and I...we weren't close. In truth, she was only arranged to me to give me heirs for the throne, but soon after we married, she..." I cleared my throat. "She passed away," I said. "However, this was not before she gave me someone very important and dear to my heart."

I felt the girl tense as she learned this, and I could anticipate that she was now very nervous.

We strode through to the connecting corridor that led into my daughter's palace, and I led her through the halls to a large, lavish playroom where I knew my daughter was hosting the children of the nobles who had come for the banquet.

She wasn't aware of what was going on or the purpose of the banquet, but she knew there was a party.

As the princess, she hosted tea parties for the nobles' children during these events to gain her own social standing in high society.

She noted my presence, even as I had my wife hide behind the wall.

"Papa!" My daughter cried, rushing over to me. "Papa, they told me that you were getting a new wife!" She cried, sobbing and throwing herself into my arms. "That isn't the reason for this party, right? I told them they were all crazy! There is no way you would bring another woman here!"

I cringed, and she felt my tension when I didn't answer right away.

"P...papa...?" She asked, crying harder. "Papa, tell me it isn't true!" She sobbed.

I pulled away, and I reached forward to my new bride, bringing her to stand in view.

The interpreter quickly told her the situation.

She gazed around the room before settling her eyes on my daughter, looking at her with trepidation in her eyes.

The other children gasped and bowed, but *my* daughter, proud and arrogant, stood there gaping at me as if I had just done the vilest of crimes before her.

"Princess Conlaed, I would like to introduce you to the newly instated empress...her majesty, Empress Nieves Eirwen Abeloth."

Conlaed's face turned furious even as her body became rigid.

"You're lying!" She cried, pointing at my bride, who cringed under the weight of my daughter's shouts, eyes wide and not understanding. "That girl is barely older than I am! How old is she, ten? There's no way *she's* your wife!" My daughter cried.

"*Hold your tongue!*" I shouted, and my daughter flinched hard, gaping at me as if I had slapped her.

That was reasonable, though, considering that I had never shouted at her even once in her life...

She glared at the empress, practically snarling. "**You**!" She growled. "You made my papa shout at me!"

When the empress gaped at the interpreter, my daughter continued on, realizing the situation.

"A foreigner!? She's a foreigner who can't even understand us!" She cried. "She must be thinking we're savages!"

"Conlaed, stop this nonsense," I said, rubbing my temples and knelt down to her level. "Princess, darling…this was my duty, a necessary action for me as the emperor. Whether you like it or not, the empress is my wife, now, and as such, she is your step-mother. I fully expect for you to be nice to her. She will learn quickly and will be a good empress for the empire. I want for you to be kind to her and help her learn. I expect nothing less from my princess," I said, swiping a hand beneath her chin and poking her nose.

She giggled and I took her into a hug. "Yes, papa."

"I know you will be a good princess, right?" I asked, and she nodded. "Right, then. You know you will always be daddy's princess," I smiled at her, and she clung to me tightly. "Now, go on and play with your friends. I will come and see you again later."

"Yes, papa," she said, glaring at my bride before she ran off to play with the other children.

I sighed, shutting the door and leading Nieves through the halls again. "This is the princess's palace, as you may have guessed. She is hotheaded and spoiled, but she is a good kid. I sort of over-pampered her when her mother passed away, and I tried to compensate for her not having a mother around."

The interpreter told her, and she spoke to him, a longing look on her face.

"'She is lucky to have you. How old is she?'"

"She is eight," I said. "She is coming close to her ninth birthday, soon."

She looked a bit depressed, and I remembered hearing that her father had passed away just a year ago.

It must still be fresh in her mind, and I felt pity for her as I thought of my relationship with my own daughter.

She may have been close to him, and had been sent here to be my bride only a year after he had died.

She was probably missing him.

"Is there anything you would particularly like to see, before I show you around?" I asked, and she contemplated when the interpreter asked.

"She said that she would like to see the library," I was told.

I smiled. "Not much to do in the north, hm? I don't know many girls your age who spend much time reading," I chuckled. "However, we have a large library in the central palace. Would you like to see that first?"

The interpreter asked her, and she nodded, and I gave a slight bow. "Alright, then."

"I will take her, your majesty," he said. "In the meantime, I encourage you to bring in a second interpreter," he smiled at me. "She has mentioned that she would like to learn the language of the south, so it would be good if you could meet her effort...if you don't mind my opinion."

I laughed. "You practically read my mind. I have already made a mental note to do so."

He bowed, turning and leading my empress through the halls to the library, and I made my way back to my office, where my butler waited for me.

"Your majesty! I thought you would be enjoying the banquet, still."

"I need for you to bring in a second interpreter," I told him. "And I want to bring in the captains of the knight units to choose an escort for the empress."

Chapter 5 — Nieves

I sat in the library, reading over some translation books that I found.

I discovered that this was how my interpreter had first started learning my language, before he had moved to the north for some years to become fluent.

So far, my husband seemed…far *kinder* than I had expected.

Though I knew that he didn't intend to interact with me a lot until I was older, that in itself brought me a bit of comfort. If I stayed out of his way and didn't bother him, I was sure everything would be fine.

I perked up when I saw the interpreter step into the room, bringing me a small piece of cake.

"I saw that you didn't eat a lot earlier, and I thought you may enjoy some dessert."

I beamed at him. "Thank you," I smiled, taking the plate.

It had been over two years since I had eaten any cake.

When I had turned ten, and the servants were preparing a birthday party and cakes for the celebration as father took me to the power summit…I had been so looking forward to having cake with my new snow wyvern.

However, there had been no reason to celebrate, and the party had been cancelled. I hadn't had cake since.

I smiled bitterly as I took a bite, and though the taste wasn't something that I was accustomed to as there was a kick of spices that I wasn't adjusted to eating yet, it still tasted good.

"Thank you," I told him. "It is good."

"It is a traditional spice cake of the empire," he said. "And, it happens to be the emperor's favorite cake."

I smiled. "He seems nicer than I had expected."

He laughed. "He can be terrifying, but he is generally kind to women. He probably thinks of you similarly to his own daughter, or perhaps a little sister? That is just my guess, though."

"May I…ask what happened?" I asked. "With the former empress, I mean. I don't mean to pry, but I feel it is odd that the former empress died so young. Did…did he kill her?"

He rubbed the back of his head, a bit nervous. "Well…there *are* rumors that her death was caused by him, but there was no official evidence or investigation. Their relationship wasn't a particularly happy one. She was nineteen when he was twelve, and it was reported throughout the kingdom that suddenly, even at that young age, the empress was pregnant.

"When they announced it together to the city, he…he looked nauseated. I remember watching him look almost sickened, even as he followed her around like a lost puppy. I believe she tried to hold authority over him and manipulate him with her older age and the fact that she had taken his innocence. Honestly, I don't think it happened under pleasant circumstances. Though, we aren't actually supposed to talk about the former empress," he said, clearing his throat. "His majesty doesn't like hearing about her. The only reason I gave a brief explanation is because I am speaking in a language they do not understand. I wouldn't dare to speak of her in my native tongue."

I considered this, wondering if there was a manner in which I could bring it up to him without angering him.

"The princess...seemed very upset," I said, remembering how she had pointed and shouted at me, glaring daggers with her sharp eyes.

He nodded. "The princess is well known for her clinginess to the emperor," he said, smiling. "He has doted on her quite thoroughly because her mother...was very unhappy that she was born a girl. The empress had one good shot to give the emperor a son, you see. She sort of...*forced* her hand, and after that, the emperor kept a strong watch over it. She didn't have another chance to catch him off guard again."

"Oh," I said, surprised. "I see..."

"You, my lady, were born after a brother, thus, your father likely wasn't bothered by your gender. However, the entire reason that the former empress had been wed to the emperor after the death of his father was to give him an heir and bring honor to her house as a successful empress. But that didn't go well, when she birthed a daughter instead of a son."

"I see..."

"The advisors may have insisted on his majesty marrying again, but he chose his bride himself. He wanted someone young, who he could grow to know slowly over time, rather than being forced into a romantic relationship right away."

I started to understand, then, that this was the reason he hadn't been close to the former empress.

She had been forced as his bride, and she was already old enough to bear heirs for him.

He had likely been made to bed her even though he was so young.

He was manipulated and gaslighted to be attached to her, with her having taken his innocence from him and being the only one to have him in such a way. He would remember her as his first for the rest of his life.

He likely hadn't had any choice.

I felt my heart tug. It was no different than a young woman being forced to be with an older man.

"I...I won't have to enter a romantic relationship with him right away?" I asked, a bit nervous.

He smiled. "No. He has been very clear about his intentions to wait until you have gotten a bit older to enter that kind of relationship with you. He just wanted you to have time to enjoy the palace life and learn your other duties as empress before you two became intimately involved. If anything, he would prefer not to be closely involved with you yet, and let things just happen naturally over time. There is no pressure for either of you, here."

I smiled at his consideration, but that also worried me more.

Would that mean that I would be killed before I ever got to have such an experience?

If he discovered that his bride had tricked him and he wasn't even being intimate with me, he would have no viable reason to let me live...or, to not send me back home if he was merciful enough to let me live.

"Okay, so there is something I wish to say to him myself," I told him, and he helped me go through the sentence and learn it in my own voice even as I finished my spice cake.

The rest of the evening passed without seeing him—which didn't surprise me, now that I knew the situation—before I was led to his chambers. I had already been informed that we would be sharing connected rooms.

His room was the one connected to the foyer that led to the hall, and you had to go through his room to reach the door that opened to my bedroom.

Through my room, there were doors that led to a balcony that looked out to the ocean beyond the mountains.

I stood outside, and I jumped in surprise when the emperor, butler and someone I didn't know stepped up to the door.

The emperor spoke to the man I didn't know, and he bowed and turned to me, bowing again.

"His majesty says, 'welcome to your new chambers. I hope you find them comfortable. Let the staff know if there is anything that you need at any time.' I would like to say it is an honor to meet you, your majesty," he said, giving a bow. "I am Ash, an interpreter who can speak four languages fluently, and I was just hired on to teach his majesty your language so that he can communicate with you personally. Please have patience as I teach him."

I gave a small curtsy. "Thank you," I smiled softly at him. "I appreciate your hard work."

He looked surprised, and began talking excitedly to my husband, who smiled warmly at me.

Then, he glanced to me. "I was praising you. It is quite unusual for nobles, particularly from the north, to be kind and warm to the staff—or anyone, for that matter. It is an honor to work with you!" He said, cheerful.

Then, we turned to the room as the butler opened the doors for us, and I gazed in awe of the luxurious space.

It was even fancier than my room as a princess in the northern kingdom, before I had been cast away to the warehouse on the edge of the estate.

I hadn't ever seen such lavish rooms.

We entered the space together, and I could see from the corner of my eye that the emperor was watching my reaction before he led me to the double doors in the center of the wall. He opened them, and I stepped into the new room, gasping and taking in the sight.

The room was gold and pink, with tones of purple and burgundy spaced around the room. The bed was large and covered with a brilliant purple duvet with bright pink and gold patterns embroidered on it.

There was a lounging chair with the finest pink and burgundy fabric, and all of the wood work, the bed frame and dresser, the nightstands…all of it was painted white, with gold filigree.

I looked to the double glass doors that led out to the balcony, and there was even an attached bathroom in each bedroom. I glanced in, seeing a large, luxurious bath tub inside.

"Wow…" I whispered, awed. I turned to the emperor with a shocked expression, my hand fisted over my heart. "Is…this really *mine*?" I asked.

The interpreter translated, and the emperor smiled warmly, giving a slight bow.

"I hope it is to your liking," he said in my own language, and I gasped, beaming at him.

It sounded rehearsed, and it made my heart quicken a bit to know that he had practiced something to say to me in my own language.

I remembered the phrase *I* had practiced, and I stepped to him, going into a very painful but deep, reverently respectful curtsy, my head low.

"I am honored to come here to be your wife," I spoke in his language, feeling harsh and quick on my tongue. I struggled with the pronunciation, but I pushed myself to get through it.

I saw his hand as he took my chin in his hold, lifting my gaze to meet his face, and I saw the tenderness in his eyes as he smiled at me.

"Thank you," he said, giving me a deep bow.

I smiled at him, understanding that he was thanking me for speaking in his own language as much as he was thanking me for what I had said.

He gestured to a rope by the bed, and he made a tugging motion in the air, saying something to me.

"He says, 'pull this rope if you need someone, and a servant will come to you right away,'" he told me.

I bowed, and told him thank you in his own language, before I stepped over to the bed, where my two small bags of possessions sat next to it.

They all stepped out, before a woman stepped in, wearing a maid's uniform.

"I honor greet empress," she said in my language, but her tone was thick and struggling over the words. She spoke as if she were trying to speak her own tongue, but it was forced in my language harshly.

I smiled at the effort, nonetheless.

I gave a small curtsy. "Thank you," I said in her tongue, and she looked surprised before she started rambling excitedly in her language. I held up my hands quickly. "Whoa, whoa," I said. "I am still learning," I fumbled over the words in her language.

"Ohh," she smiled, giving me a warm expression. "You be good, hope you like here," she said.

I smiled at her. "Thank you."

"I bring water," she said, lifting the tray in her hands holding a glass of water. "I, Ember," she said.

I took the water from her, thanking her and taking a sip before I gasped.

The water quality was totally different than in the North. In the North, we had to take snow and boil it to purify it and make drinking water, but this tasted different.

A bit earthy, almost.

"What...kind?" I asked, trying to think of the words to ask the right question.

"Water? From well," she said.

Ah, so that was why. It was well water.

We didn't have wells in the North, so it was a completely different flavor.

Thankfully, I actually preferred this well water over the snow water in the north.

"Thank you, Ember," I told her. I glanced at my bags, and lifted one to the bed and opened it, lifting out a couple of outfits. "Help?" I asked.

She looked excited, rushing over to me and taking the clothes, putting them in the wardrobe standing nearby.

We didn't do a lot of talking, but she finished helping me put my few things away—which only consisted of two nightgowns, two dresses, and two pairs of shoes, along with a few books that I cherished and a stuffed white-fox doll that needed some repair.

I had one beautiful necklace left to me by my mother—a silver locket with a portrait of her on the inside, and the outer casing was embedded with tiny sapphires and diamonds. It was the most precious of my possessions.

My fox doll had been a gift from my father for my third birthday, and it was the only stuffed animal I had ever received. Children in the north—nobles, at least—were expected to be classy, reserved and mature. Having such toys led to immaturity; or so they believed.

I crawled up into the bed, and Ember blew out the lamps that lit the room, letting the moonlight stream in from the balcony doors and the sound of ocean waves echo into my chambers.

I tossed and turned for a while after she left, unable to fall asleep.

Finally, I stood, trudging over to the balcony doors and stepping outside.

It was a little chilly, and I shivered lightly as the wind picked up, but I could see the moon luminating the night.

It seemed that my body had already quickly adjusted to the heat of the south, for this small amount of wind to cause a chill. The south agreed with me.

I hadn't ever been fond of the harsh freezing cold of the north.

I could barely make out the ocean from this spot, but I spotted a small little iron table with two chairs sat beside it and took a seat, looking out over the railing, facing out toward the scenery.

I looked down to the left, seeing the road that led down to the city below, homes lit and lanterns lighting the path.

I heard the fading of chatter as citizens returned to their homes, and life started to settle down for the night.

A particularly strong gust of wind came as I saw a few dragons flying off in the distance, diving down into the darkness of the ocean and coming up with sizeable fish in their jaws.

I startled when a warm robe was draped over my shoulders, and I looked up to see my husband staring out into the night, one hand held high and fire shooting out into the air in bursts; a signal.

I heard the call of a dragon in the distance, and I gasped as I watched a return signal from the mountain top before a huge dark figure began to head towards us.

My husband kept his attention on the figure, waiting until the dragon had arrived and hovered, flapping his large and powerful wings to hold himself steady just below the balcony.

My husband put a foot on the railing and startled me when he leapt off into the darkness, landing swiftly and skillfully on the back of his dragon.

He spoke to the creature in the guttural, harsh dragon tongue, and I saw the dragon look to me, huff and nod his head in a way that made it seem like he was acknowledging me.

My husband finally looked up at me, holding out a hand toward me in offering, and I felt a rush run through me.

He was...offering me a ride?

I pointed at myself with a look of confusion, and he laughed lightly, beaming a childish grin up at me in my place on the balcony before he gave a nod and a small bow.

The sentence that he spoke then sounded like this: "*Eel Katchoon emprehn mahn.*"

His language was so harsh and guttural, thick and slashing…but I could almost understand what he was trying to say as he held his arms out in a catching gesture;

He would catch me…

I gulped, climbing over the railing and holding it behind me before I pushed out with my legs, feeling myself panic as I shot out into the darkness of the night.

I closed my eyes as I fell—before I felt my body land in something warm and firm, grasping onto me tightly.

I gasped, looking up at my husband as he smiled at me warmly, settling me into place in front of him with his arms wrapped around me and holding reins in his hands.

He spoke again in the dragon language, and the wings of this giant beast pushed and beat powerfully as he moved through the air.

I was breathless, almost hyperventilating in terror at first as we flew out over the city, getting further from the castle as we headed towards the ocean.

I watched in awe, feeling the wind taken from my lungs at the beauty of the ocean crashing against the mountainside on the side opposite from the palace.

I could see the balcony where we had been, illuminated by the lamps that he had carried to the doorway without my noticing it somehow.

I looked around, enjoying the feeling of the wind despite the chill.

Honestly, I could hardly feel it, with how heated his majesty was and the warmth of the dragon's scales between my legs.

Fire dragons radiated heat, just like I'd read so many years ago. It was interesting to see it for myself.

I remembered the term for "your majesty" and "emperor" that I had been taught earlier that day, so I looked over my shoulder.

"Your majesty, emperor," I spoke, and I immediately saw his bright, burning orange gaze meet mine.

"Emprehn," he spoke, though I understood this as the word for "empress."

I felt my stomach lurch to my throat as we suddenly dove, and I gasped out a cry and clung to his arms as he chuckled warmly behind me. It was a playful, yet somehow endearing sound.

We landed with a boom, and I opened my eyes and looked to see that we had landed on the sand of the beach.

The emperor slid off of the dragon, holding his waiting arms for me again as I did the same, and he caught me smoothly yet again.

I felt the smooth, still-warm sand on the soles of my feet and squishing between my toes, and I marveled at it.

I gasped, laughing and squeezing my toes, squishing my feet further into the sand and looking at him with a truly free expression.

I hadn't ever felt sand.

I hadn't felt grass, or lush forests, or warmth…

Even during the summer, the North stayed rather cold and only evergreens bloomed there in the northern mountains.

I never saw much greenery. Just gray and white from the mountains and rocks.

This...this was more than I had ever dreamed.

This man had made this happen.

He had come to check on me in the night, to see if I was sleeping, and found a young girl out on the balcony alone, shivering and chilly.

He had given her a wonderous and magical ride on a dragon—something that any other noble lady would have felt before, but I hadn't—and brought me to a beach.

I hadn't ever had an experience this wonderful.

I was scared of him and his terrifying reputation...but he didn't seem to be all bad.

In fact, he had been nothing but pleasant to me since I had arrived...but then, we hadn't known each other long. That might change in the future, for all that I knew.

He watched me with wide, surprised eyes at my boundless joy, smiling brightly at me as I laughed.

He took my hand, kneeling in the sand and pressing a small, chaste kiss to the back of my hand, looking up at me.

"Thank you," I said, and he smiled up at me brighter.

I knew he had learned those words in my language, so he knew what I had said.

"Like?" He asked, gesturing to the beach, and I nodded enthusiastically.

"You won't understand me, but I've never seen anything so beautiful as this. All I know is mountains and snow. This is…wonderful," I said, soft. "The only thing more beautiful than this view…would be you," I blushed, looking at him as he watched me intensely.

I almost wondered if he actually understood me, but that couldn't be.

He had only just gotten an interpreter for himself, so I knew that he didn't know the language yet.

I prayed that he never found out how pitiful I truly was.

He would be so disappointed.

I took in what he was wearing, and I blushed redder.

He wore a robe that left the chest visible, open loosely and showing all of his thick, soft musculature. I felt like his chest was even bigger than my own…no, I knew it.

His arms, covered by meshy sleeves, were thick and warm, muscular and dark.

His thick, wild, fiery hair was wind-blown and wild looking. His eyes were edged with dark, thick, beautiful reddish-brown eyelashes that looked almost black.

A high-bridged, proud nose with a slight inward curve, and high cheekbones.

He was a real beauty, and if he wasn't the emperor, he could go into business as the world's leading model for Southern Beauty among the Fire Drake territories. Yet somehow, he was *my husband*...

His eyes were sharp and piercing, but warm and heated.

I felt my belly heating, and I quickly looked away, out at the water.

After a while of walking in the sand and enjoying the view, I watched as he glanced toward the palace, and climbed back into his place on his dragon.

He reached his hands out for me, helping me to step up and get into place, before we flew back to the palace.

The dragon hovered upward over the balcony now, and the emperor jumped down to the balcony before I jumped to land into his arms.

He set me down into place, and led me back inside.

I took off the robe he had put on me, and he took it from me as he helped me get tucked into bed.

I felt so tired, now, after all of that work.

My eyes closed, and I felt my heart flutter as I heard a warm, amused-sounding chuckle near my head as he utterly shocked me when he pressed a warm, chaste kiss to my cheek, stroking the strands of my hair away from my face and pulling my blanket to cover my shoulder.

I heard the balcony doors click closed, before his footfalls left me, and I heard the bed in the room adjoined to mine shift as he settled into his place.

I barely peeped an eye open to see that he hadn't closed the doors between our rooms...

I smiled in spite of myself.

He seemed a bit lonely, and wasn't at all like the rumors.

I felt a painful tug in my heart as I thought that perhaps the interpreter had been right. Perhaps he really did see me like a little sister…or a daughter.

I couldn't explain this ache in my heart at the thought of such a thing.

The next few days flew by and turned into a couple of weeks quickly. Time passed without much of a difference.

During that time, I didn't see the emperor much.

He was gone by the time that I awoke, and we saw one another during the meal times, but our conversation was limited and short.

Each new day, I was woken and dressed by the maids, escorted to the dining hall where I saw the emperor seated and waiting, and we sat and ate breakfast together.

Then, he would go and take care of paperwork as I was taken through the halls on tour, or I was taken to the library for lessons in the Southern Imperial language.

I found out that after I had become fluent in the language, then I would begin undergoing tutoring to teach me about my duties as the empress and how to manage the castle and city.

I also learned that the emperor, himself, was undergoing lessons in my language.

His reasoning being that, though we wouldn't interact often for a while, he wanted to be able to communicate with me without the help of interpreters.

A couple of weeks went by without seeing one another outside of meal times, before we set it into practice.

I had been surprised to get the request to join him outside of a meal, and I was told that we would begin seeing each other more often to practice the language.

It had been almost a month since I had arrived, and as we sat at tea time, the emperor looked up at me.

"I have been learning the Northern language," he said, and I startled and gave him my attention. His voice sounded strange, trying to go over the smooth and delicate language that was my mother tongue when he was so used to a harsh and forceful language of his own people. "I have been getting guidance, I hope I am doing well."

I smiled. "You *are*, your majesty. You are doing very well. A husband would not usually bother to learn a wife's language." I smiled at him. Then, I switched to *his* language, forcing the harsh punctuation that I wasn't used to in order to help my pronunciations and accent. "Thank you for your thoughtfulness. I have also been learning, and I hope I am speaking this well, also."

His eyes widened in surprise, and he laughed as he beamed a smile at me, clapping. "*You* have learned fast," he said. "I will try harder. Let's see who speaks who's language faster."

I laughed at the competition. "It is a contest, then?"

He barked out a happy laugh. "Yes, *everything* is contest in the South," he said, smiling at me. Then, he switched back to his own language. "How have you been faring so far?"

"I am enjoying life here, your majesty. Thank you. Is there anything coming up that I need to prepare for?" I asked, already aware but wanting to keep talking to him.

He nodded. "Princess Conlaed is hosting a tea party in two days, and you are on the guest list. It will be your first tea party in the South."

The only reason that I understood this was because the interpreter had actually practiced saying that phrase to me earlier during my lesson that morning.

He had heard the news, and had alerted me right away that the emperor would be informing me at our tea time together.

As empress, it was my duty to attend the tea parties hosted by the princess in order to build a bond, and to help manage the event as a chaperone.

It was also a chance to meet nobles of the south, and therefore somewhat be introduced into the society of this country.

Normally, an empress would have been older than I was, so I would have already had my social debut at a formal event, but this was an informal way to get my name and impression out among the nobles.

It was a casual social debut, if you will.

If the nobles favored me, I was a lot more likely to have an easier time settling into the empire and having respect. It was of great importance to do well during the tea party.

The interpreter and a tutor had already gone over all of the things that I would need to know, and we were going to be holding a practice tea-party the following day during my lessons.

I gave a nod, letting him know that I understood. "Yes, that is important. I will be there and I won't let you down," I beamed at him, and he gave me a warm expression and tender smile.

"Thank you," he said, soft.

Suddenly, an advisor burst into the room and rushed to the emperor, whispering something that I couldn't make out into his ear, and he gaped at the advisor with a hard expression before he turned to me, a serious expression on his face.

"I must attend to some important business. Please, continue your tea." He stood, leaving the room in haste.

What had that been about…?

I glanced to the butler as he entered the room, cleaning up the emperor's place.

"What is happening?" I asked, a bit worried.

"Oh," he said, a hesitant look on his face. "The princess is upset that you will be in attendance to her tea party," he said meekly. "She is throwing a tantrum in her room."

I felt pain spear my heart.

I knew that the princess was only four years younger than I was, currently, and she resented me for a number of reasons.

The top reason being that now, she was no longer the only girl in her father's life, and *I wasn't even old enough to be her mother*.

Her father, himself, was *barely* old enough to be her father. Had he been a girl, he wouldn't have been able to get pregnant with her at that age more than likely.

I was twelve, and I still had yet to even start my monthly cycles.

I knew she must resent me the most because I was only a few years older than she, but I held such a powerful rank that I didn't deserve.

I was just a washed up, worthless dud of a princess from the north.

What right did I have to be an empress of the south? To be here, living a decent life, playing house and mommy to a girl just a few years younger than I...?

Chapter 6 – Nieves

February, 722 Fire Drake Dynasty

I looked to the gown that had been prepared for me for the tea party, twirling so that I could see it better in the mirror.

It was the day of my step-daughter's tea party, and I knew that she didn't want me there.

I felt my nerves rumbling in my belly, but I tried to push it down and ignore them.

As a princess of the north, I'd only held *one* tea party—and it had only been amongst the children of the nobles at the highest bracket in the north.

That had been when I was seven, five whole years ago.

This was not only a tea party, but it was also the princess's birthday, and she had personally asked to hold a tea party to celebrate.

So, as the empress who was expected to participate and chaperone but the hated step-mother who wasn't actually invited as anything more than an obligation, I had mixed feelings.

I wanted to get along with the princess. I knew that she saw me as a threat, an obstacle getting between her and her father…but I didn't intend to take that place from her.

I sighed, putting on the hat that was chosen for me, and I looked at myself.

I looked like a real southern noble, now, with the exception of my physical features.

I stuck out like a sore thumb among the dark, tanned people with their red and blonde and fiery orange hair colors, and their golden, orange or red eye colors.

I would never get lost in a crowd, I mused softly, laughing beneath my breath.

A knock sounded, and I saw the emperor standing there in a uniform that matched my gown.

As my husband, he was obligated to match my outfit and escort me to any and all imperial functions. If he were to refuse, it would be a catastrophe, as well as a huge sign that I was not accepted as the empress.

Him showing up to escort me was a very good sign.

"You look lovely," he said, smiling and dipping in a small bow. "You will do well," he said. He held his arm out for me, and I took it, letting him escort me.

Husbands escorted their wives like this, I had learned.

I hadn't learned a lot about this in the north, because I was so young. Courting mannerism didn't start being taught to noble ladies until age ten, but yet again, because of my circumstances…I hadn't been able to learn.

I was learning quite a lot here, it seemed.

He led me through the halls to the connecting junction, where we came to enter the princess's palace.

There was already a large group of nobles congregating there, and they all bowed and murmured out greetings as we approached.

"It is an honor to greet the emperor and empress," one of the dignitaries said. "My daughter is already inside, your majesty," he said, glancing at me.

"I will see you here later," Kai said, smiling at me. "I hope you have fun."

He pressed a kiss to my hand as I gave a curtsy, and the guards opened the door for me to enter into the tea party space as my husband started talking to the other nobles gathered in the parlor.

As I stepped inside, the soft gasps and murmurs alerted me that they had noticed my entrance; they stood from their places, giving curtsies while the servants bowed, and I was led to my place at the table of royalty.

I had learned, the day before, that there would be several tables gathered together in a circle, and they would be set up in three groupings; the royalty, the higher-ranked nobles, and the lower-ranked nobles.

There were several visiting nobles from close nations, and you could clearly tell their nationalities from their clothing and the pendants they wore on their clothing.

There was a princess from the earth city, and a duchess from the air city.

"It is so nice to meet you, your majesty," the princess from the earth city said. She spoke my tongue fluently, and I was pleasantly surprised. "When I had heard that the emperor was remarrying, I was quite surprised—he hadn't intended to marry, but then they brought in a princess from the snow kingdom! It was quite a shock. But the south seems to suit you, you look well."

"I do enjoy the warmer temperature, and thank you for your kind words," I said, bowing my head slightly. "Thank you for making the journey all this way for this tea party. I know that this is a great feat from personal experience. We actually passed by the earth and air kingdoms on the way from the north, and so we appreciate this effort on behalf of this event."

They turned to the doors as the princess was announced, and her father let go of her hand at the doors, letting her come in.

Ah, I thought. *He had gone to get her after he had dropped me off so that he could escort her separately. He was her father, after all.*

The thought made my throat feel tight.

All that I had seen when I saw them together was him being warm and caring and doting towards her.

I wished that I'd had that kind of relationship with my own father, and my heart tugged painfully. I grieved for the relationship that was possible between a father and daughter, but I never had.

Even before my lack of powers had been revealed, we hadn't been particularly close. Families in the north were just as cold as the snow and ice they lived surrounded by, or so that was the rumor.

I could attest to the rumors being mostly true, especially among the royalty and nobles of the north. I was sure the commoners weren't so cold, but the nobility had to maintain frigid standards.

I gave a small, elegant bend towards the princess, spreading my gown's skirt without going into a full curtsy.

"Welcome, Princess Conlaed."

She hesitated, but when the people around us started to whisper, she glared at me and gave a small curtsy in return. "Thank you...step-mother." She was led to her place, and we all sat for the servants to being bringing out the teas and pastries.

"So, your majesty, you must have a special bond with the princess," one of the older members of the royal table sneered at me, and I felt my tension rise a bit.

I could sense underlying hostility, but I didn't know who this noblewoman even was.

Though, from her golden blonde hair and her bright, blazing orange eyes, she was quite obviously from the Fire Drake empire.

I smiled at her. "I haven't had much of a chance to get close to her, as of yet."

She chuckled. "Oh, so you must not care to get to be on good terms with the princess, then? How does the emperor feel about that?"

I heard several other Fire empire ladies murmuring softly, and I glanced at my glass of tea as a servant put a couple of sugar cubes into my cup of tea.

I lifted my glass, *trying* to remain dignified.

"That isn't it," I said, smiling to the lady. "I have been busy undergoing lessons to learn the fire empire's language, and I am still learning as I'm not fluent yet. I want to be fluent before I make a blunder in front of my step-daughter by messing up her mother tongue."

I took a sip of my tea as a sour look crossed the woman's face, only for her to sneer and chuckle again when I felt my face tighten.

It hadn't been sugar cubes placed into my tea, but rather, it had been cubes of *salt*...

This was my first test.

I remembered my interpreter having warned me of this the day before; he had told me that, often times, if a noble lady had a personal dispute toward me or disliked me, she would bribe a servant to give me salt cubes rather than sugar.

This was a large insult, but also a test, to see how I handled myself as a noblewoman.

Thus, it was a challenge; did I storm out in a rage?

Did I throw a tantrum and ruin the tea party for all?

Accuse random ladies without *proof*?

Or, did I not respond at all and bend to their whims by letting them walk all over me...?

As empress, I had a duty to uphold grace but not to let others step all over my dignity. I had to respond, in some way, but I needed to approach the situation with caution.

I remembered my interpreter's suggestion, and I simply smiled at the lady whom I had assumed had bribed the servant.

Then, I turned to the servants, and I called them over.

It was considered very rude to not finish a cup of tea in this kingdom, as it was an insult to the host.

The host whom, of all people, happened to be my step-daughter. Considering the precursor to this, the topic of discussion, I could easily tell without much need for outside assistance…

I was being set up to insult my step-daughter.

I drank the cup of tea, *quickly*, ignoring the sting of salty hot tea running down my throat as I tried to forego tasting it, and smiled to the servant.

"Might I have another cup?" I asked. "That was refreshing," I smiled. I glanced at the girl out of my peripheral, trying to gauge *her* response to *my* response.

She startled minutely; just enough to let me know that she was surprised by the request, *and* that let me know that *she knew* the cubes were salt. She was the culprit.

I looked to the maid, who also startled slightly, and I realized that this was the maid who had been bribed to put the salt cubes in, or else she'd have no reason to panic.

So, these two were the conspirators.

She shakily poured me another cup of tea, and I covered the top when she went to add more cubes to my tea.

"No more for me, thank you," I smiled at her brightly, turning instead to my plate of macaroons, and I took one and dipped it into my tea before I took a bite.

I saw some ladies gasping, surprised by this unusual move.

"You dipped the macaroon?" One lady whispered, surprised.

I smiled at her. "Ah, yes. This was common in the snow drake kingdom, as hot drinks were often used to heat sweet treats to make them warm our bodies. It is cold there, of course. It is just habit."

That was an excuse, but it was a truthful one.

I had done that to show that I could forge my own answer to an insult, and I noticed the princess glaring at me as well as the lady who had insulted me before.

Why was the princess angry?

Perhaps they were in on the insult together...?

The rest of the tea party went without any hitches, and once it was over, I remembered my final duty as a chaperone to the party, standing and giving a small curtsy at the door, facing everyone.

"Thank you all very much for attending this tea party," I said. "I hope that you have enjoyed yourselves. A bright and happy birthday to the princess," I said, lifting my cup of tea and downing it in a gulp even as they all murmured out congratulations and happy birthdays to the princess while I stepped out of the room.

The emperor stood there, hand out in offering to mine. I took his hand, letting him lead me through the corridor and back to the main palace.

"Did you enjoy yourself, empress?" He asked, glancing at me sideways.

I smiled. "Mostly," I smiled.

"Mostly?" He asked. "What is wrong?"

I laughed softly. "I was tested a bit. One of the attendees bribed a servant to give me salt cubes for my tea. I handled it well, though, and I brought honor to you as my husband without making a fuss."

He took a deep breath, looking perturbed. "I thought that may happen, but I had *hoped* that it wouldn't," he said, seeming to feel guilty. "I think I know the culprit."

"I believe that it was the golden-haired lady," I said.

"Hm?" He asked. "I...I was going to say that I thought it was princess Conlaed. Did you have issues with someone else?"

"There was a lady—older than the rest of us, but not older than her early twenties—who had golden hair and orange eyes, and she was openly hostile toward me in conversation."

"What did she say?" He said, tone suddenly cold.

I shivered a bit involuntarily, feeling the air turn hot with his question, but I felt like I was in ice.

"She first questioned my bond with the princess. I told her I hadn't been able to spend much time with the princess yet, and she said that I must not care to get close to Princess Conlaed and..." I swallowed, glancing at him. "She sneered and asked me how *you* felt about that." I sighed, looking at my feet. "I told her that wasn't how I felt, that I was still learning the language and I want to speak fluently before getting close to the princess so I didn't mess up. Then, I was given the salt cubes in my tea."

He gave a slow, acknowledging nod, before he startled me when he turned, rushing back towards the room here the tea party was...*and pulling me right along with him.*

Startled, my feet struggled to keep up as he walked at a fast pace.

We saw the servants and guards looking rather nervous as we came back, and some even fell on their faces, terrified and trembling.

When we reached the tea-party space and saw the nobles leaving, they all gasped when they saw us, bowing and murmuring softly, wondering why we had returned.

"*Faiza Von Blaze,*" The emperor addressed, his voice a blast of hot rage, and an entire group of golden-haired people fell to their knees, gaping at the lady who had insulted me. He stepped up with me, hand in hand, to stand before the lady. "I was informed that you showed disrespect to my empress."

"It wasn't me!" She cried. "I didn't give her the salt cubes!"

"Which undoubtedly means that you at least *knew* about it, and therefore, are guilty by association, because *that* wasn't even what I was referring to. I heard that you sneered at my bride, and that you asked her *how I felt* about her standing with the princess."

She gaped up at me, before turning her fearful gaze to my husband. "I...I didn't realize that I wasn't supposed to—"

"How *I* feel about *anything*, least of all about *my* wife's relationship with *my* daughter is no concern of yours. Your blatant snickering and sneering is an obvious insult and disrespect. Had you behaved in such a way toward the princess or myself, you would have been beheaded on the spot, so why did you think you could behave in such a way to the *empress*? Is it because you are backed by the princess, who is openly admitted to dislike the empress?"

She sputtered, glancing at the princess who stood nearby, looking on in horror.

I could see it, now.

She had been caught.

The emperor glanced to the guards, giving a nod, and the guard pulled out a sword as the girl cried and grasped onto my husband, begging for mercy.

"W-wait!" I said, stepping between the girl and the guard. I turned to my husband, who cocked his head in a questioning way, a look of surprised confusion on his face. "S-she doesn't need to *die* for this. It wasn't a grave insult, and I handled the situation well enough. I didn't tell you so that you would kill her…"

He glanced at the girl, before glancing back at me. "*Do you know who this girl is?*" He asked, looking at her again. "She is the girl whom the council of advisors *wanted* to arrange my marriage with, before I insisted on bringing in a girl from another kingdom."

I startled, glancing at her in a new light. That…

She was jealous of me, I realized. *She had thought that she would be empress…at least, until I had been brought in and had taken her position.*

"Thus, she was deliberately sneering and snickering at you and asking you how I felt because she was looking down on you for your position as my empress. Salt cubes aside, she was still blatantly rude. I am insulted by this rudeness, because she is therefore being disrespectful to me."

"But beheading is a drastic reaction," I said, softly, but I stood firm.

He gave me a frustrated expression, making an exasperated sound, and turning away from the scene. "Fine. You come up with a suitable punishment, then," he said, and everyone around us gasped and gaped.

They looked as if they had never thought it possible that their emperor wasn't executing someone over an insult...

Perhaps it hadn't ever been possible before.

She clung to my feet, thanking me for my mercy, and crying as she trembled.

I straightened, determined to put as much authority into my command as possible. "Take the lady to the dungeon. I sentence her to a month in prison, and ban her from attending any social events for three years...which I will lessen to a single year if you confirm your backer," I said.

She glanced to the princess. "P-princess Conlaed...told me that she would protect me if I bribed the servants to give you salt cubes. She has been talking to me for some time to complain about you and your position as empress...I have letters at home to prove it."

I glanced to the emperor, and he gave a small nod, granting permission. Then, I glanced nearby to a soldier. "Go to her estate and retrieve the letters to prove the princess's guilt. I will leave the situation from this point forward in his hands." I looked to the guards. "Take the lady to the dungeon. Her sentence will be reviewed again when the evidence she mentioned is brought forward."

The princess gasped, pointing at me. "Papa, you can't take her side! She shouldn't even be here! She isn't even the real empress yet! You were the one who made me do this when you told me I had to invite her to my birthday tea party!" She cried, crossing her arms and turning away.

I gaped, turning and glancing at my husband, who stood there, face sad before he gave a disappointed sigh and shook his head, bothered and obviously upset.

"Is that a blatant admission of guilt?" He asked, glancing to me before he looked to the guards. "The princess is now to be held in her room under supervision. She is suspended until further notice."

"S-s-suspended?!" She cried, whirling to look at her father. "But-but *papa*!"

"You have insulted your step-mother, and you have also insulted me. You have sullied our family name with your petty behavior. I may extend endless doting and love to you, but I am disappointed and ashamed by your actions. You are not acting like a princess." He glanced to me.

"But, papa—!"

"And to say that she isn't the real empress is not only deeply insulting, but it is very wrong of you. She is too *young* to perform nightly duties, and that is of no consequence to me as we have time for that. However, *that is not your business*, and you have no right to speak of it. You are too young to be discussing matters of intimate relations in the bedroom, anyway," he said.

"Papa—"

"*Enough!*" He shouted, shrugging her off. "You are suspended for a month."

"A month?!" She cried.

"Three months," he corrected.

"But papa—"

"*Six months!*" He said, glaring at her, and she clamped her mouth closed, giving a deep curtsy instead. "I will reduce it back to three if you apologize—*sincerely*—to the empress."

She gaped at him, but as her mouth opened to protest, he turned his head to the side and rose his eyebrows; an expression that read, "*do you want to try me again?*"

She took a deep, shaky breath, and turned to me, her body trembling softly. She gave a deep curtsy, staring at the floor.

"I am very sorry for my disrespect, emp—"

"*Look someone in the eyes when you apologize to them, Conlaed,*" her father said in a cold tone, arms crossed.

She trembled harder, and she looked up at me with eyes filled with tears and grit her teeth together, cheeks flaming red as her friends and other dignitaries had been watching the entire time. Now, they would see the spoiled princess humble herself before the empress she hated.

Her new step-mother.

"I am very sorry to have disrespected you, your majesty the empress. I have been jealous of the attention that my papa has been giving you. It was wrong of me. I apologize."

I saw some of the tension leave the emperor's body, and I realized that this wasn't him being harsh just because he was upset...he didn't just feel disrespected.

He felt upset that his daughter was refusing to get along with me.

I looked back to the princess, and I gave a deeper curtsy, spreading my skirt and bowing my head. "I accept your apology, princess Conlaed," I said. "I really, truly hope that we can get along better in the future."

She grated her teeth again, turning and running off down the hall, and I glanced to the emperor.

"I am sorry, my empress…at least, this time, you got an apology."

"It is alright," I smiled.

"It is *not* alright," he said, serious. "It is important to me that you two get along. How can we be a family if there is discord?" He asked, and I looked at him, awed.

Offering me a sincere apology—genuinely sorry or not—showed that she was at least willing to offer me an apology and that we may actually be able to bond.

It was important to him that his daughter have a good relationship with his wife, whomever she was.

I had been told, from the beginning, that I wouldn't be harmed if I didn't harm his treasures; his daughter, and his dragon.

Though, I didn't want to have any problems with her, anyway. She was just a girl who only had her father, and she saw it like I was taking her father from her.

If I had refused to get along with her, he likely would have already gotten rid of me.

He wasn't known as a tyrant for no reason.

However, for her to directly admit that she was blatantly disrespecting me? That meant that all of the drama was completely created on her end, when I hadn't done anything to cause it.

"Alright," he said, glancing to me. "All of you may disperse, now. Thank you all for coming and participating in the tea party and for the wonderful gifts for the princess in honor of her birthday."

All of the crowd that had gathered started to dissipate, and the emperor bowed and raised my hand to his lips, pressing a kiss to the back of my hand.

"I am sorry about this," he said, looking almost...bashful. He smiled. "I have a temper."

I smiled. "Thank you," I said. Then, in my own tongue, I spoke again, soft. "That...felt kind of nice."

He grinned at me. "What felt nice?"

I laughed. "You have improved the flow of speech," I said. "Much better. Your accent is getting closer." Then, I blushed. "It felt nice...for you to get angry on my behalf. I've never had anyone defend me before. It made me feel important."

I watched his ears turn slightly pink, and he looked away, so I couldn't see his face.

"Is that because you never got out while you were in the north?"

I gaped at him. "P-pardon?"

"I...I went to the interpreter, that night we went to the beach, and told them the phrase that you had said. How you know nothing but mountains and snow, never knowing anything as beautiful as that night...the only thing more beautiful...being *me*," he said, his cheeks flaming red as he turned his bright, blazing orange gaze onto me.

In this lighting, I could see bright golden flecks sparkling around the outer part of the irises, and there was dark red just outside of the pupils.

His eyes...were absolutely beautiful, like burning embers around a bed of rubies around his pupils.

He caught me staring, and blushed even darker.

He cleared his throat. "I will defend you, if you are in the right. And so far, you haven't done anything wrong. The princess has been hateful with hostile intent, and it isn't right when you didn't do anything to deserve it."

"Thank you, your majesty."

"I wish for you two to be close," he said. "I know it will take some time, but she needs a mother, and though you are close in age, I hope that you will be able to at least offer her some guidance and womanly...comfort and advice," he said.

"I will do my best," I said. "I just hope we can move past this, and that things will get better from here. It is important for us to be close, so that we can grow...as a family," I said. "I want a family."

He glanced at me, a sobering expression on his handsome face.

Chapter 7 – Kai

April, 722 Fire Drake Dynasty

Two months passed, and the empress and I had been doing much better at communicating more fluently in both of our languages during meal times and tea times.

I still didn't see her a lot outside of those scheduled meetings, but I made sure to make those times available to her, at least.

We had gotten in a habit of speaking in *her* mother tongue when we were around other people, but talking in *my* native language when we were alone.

It helped us get a lot of practice.

Since the princess had been suspended, I had only been visiting the princess once a week rather than every day; so, I instead used that extra time to start spending more time with my young empress.

I hadn't originally intended to spend this much time with the empress, but it had just seemed to work out this way. She was so different from other women I had been around…so much like a timid little bunny.

I didn't know why, but I just wanted to protect her but gobble her up all at the same time. I didn't understand these feelings.

As for the situation with the princess, this wasn't simply a way to teach the princess that her actions had consequences and to make her truly regret her actions, but it was also a way to get some more time to bond with empress Nieves.

The truth was that at the beginning of March, my informant that I had planted in the North had been spying on the northern kingdom and had taken many notes about the rumors and whispers in regards to my young wife.

It turned out that she was not simply harboring her drake companion—wyvern or amphiptere, in regards to the drake types available in that region—in the north.

The truth was that she, in fact, didn't actually *have* a companion to begin with.

I had learned that she had been taken to the summit in the north, but rather than unlocking her powers…she hadn't had any.

That didn't make sense, though, I thought. *Both of her parents were high-born nobles in the north, and all of the noble bloodlines had these abilities.*

After she had been discovered to be powerless, she had been sent into seclusion on the estate. There were no records of how she had been treated during that time or how she had lived, but it was obvious enough in the fact that they isolated her away from the public; her lack of powers and a drake companion were not favorable to their royal family.

I had married a girl who was a princess in title only, and hadn't been likely had been treated as a princess in quite some time.

I felt that, had I known this beforehand, I would have resented them and hated them for almost "*tricking*" me, by sending me a girl who had no value to them.

Now, however...now, I didn't care about her previous standing or what they thought of her, because I had gotten to know her as a person.

I knew that she was a sweet, polite young lady who was warm...*much warmer than one would think for a princess of the north.*

Now, I realized why she was so warm. She was probably so kind and warm because she didn't want to treat others the way she had likely been treated.

It bothered me, really.

I was still waiting for confirmation from my spies on this, but I had a hunch that her circumstances weren't good.

To be honest, since she had gotten to be fluent in my tongue and she had started her lessons in being an empress, she was doing a great job.

She was now learning how to manage the palace and the city, learning how to go about handling taxes and salaries for the servants.

She was learning all of her duties well.

There was only *one* duty that she hadn't started to learn, yet, and that was because I would be teaching her myself, when she got old enough...

Speaking of bedding...I also learned that not having a drake companion was likely a big portion of the reason that she had yet to start her menstrual cycles.

For a noble woman to become an adult, she had to unlock her powers and she would begin her cycles only after she had claimed her power and her companion.

It was my wizard's theory that her bloodlines were keeping her from being able to produce heirs because she was a "dud".

It seemed that the bloodline knew that she didn't have powers, and so it wouldn't pass the defect to the next generation by taking the ability to have children from her.

If *that* were truly the case, however...*that would mean that she could not bear me any children, let alone a son.*

I didn't want to send her back to the north.

As cold and frigidly heartless as they were, if I sent her back...*it would likely be a death sentence for her.*

I had to consider the options carefully.

I told my informant to burn the information, pretend he had never heard it, and to never let anyone who spoke of it live.

I couldn't let the word get out that she was powerless, because that in itself would push the council to try to select a new bride for me.

Already married or not, they would send her back to her homeland without fail if they caught wind of it.

I would have to slaughter them all to stop it, and that would drastically negatively affect my standing as emperor.

I had already made my decision, however;

Nieves was my empress, and she would stay in that position.

I had no intention of replacing her.

I glanced up from my book, and noticed her staring out at the beach again, wrapped in a sheer red shawl over her thin maroon dress.

She looked good in the southern colors, I thought.

"Nieves," I said, and she turned to me, still out on the balcony. "Would you like to go for a ride? It has been a while."

She brightened, a grin in place on her lips, and I beamed back at her.

That was a yes.

I stepped outside with her, shooting a couple of fire blasts into the air to signal my dragon.

He returned the signal, flying over to the balcony, and it was much like that first night that I had given her a ride.

She dropped into my arms before I sat her into place, and I felt her laugh with exhilaration as we took off for the beach.

When we landed, she slid down into my arms but rather than running around like a silly child, she grabbed my hands and pulled me into a trot, taking off for the water.

I laughed as we got our feet wet, and I had to help her stand in place as the strong pulling sensation of the waves on our feet almost sent her tumbling off of her feet. She reached to wrap her arms around my waist, and I chuckled as she laughed heartily as the waves pushed and sucked at her feet.

"It feels so strange!" She laughed.

In that moment, she looked up at me, beaming a smile, and the sunlight hit her in a way that made her hair shine brighter than snow, reminding me of sun shining on a patch of snow-covered field, white everywhere.

Her eyes, that stormy gray with a touch of blue around the pupil and a dark, stormy color flecked around the iris...she was stunning.

Her petite build, her heart-shaped face, her thick, sweet lips in a beautiful, pale pink color with almost a lavender shade.

She was beautiful.

I leaned forward, surprising her and her eyes going wide, as I pressed the most chaste of kisses to her lips, marveling at how soft they were.

She gasped, touching her lips and gazing up at me.

Her cheeks flushed so dark that I thought all the blood in her body must have rushed to those cheeks.

"...Empress..." I whispered, taking a step away and getting out of the water.

She trudged out with me, watching me with careful eyes.

"Are you...alright?" She asked.

I smiled. "I was fixing to ask *you* that."

She touched her lips, blushing again. "I...liked it," she said, soft.

I could barely hear her over the roaring of the waves. She glanced at me again, and stepped over to me, looking up at me with a hesitant gaze.

I smiled, and gave a soft chuckle. "Do you want another kiss?" I teased, and she blushed.

"I would like that," she said. "But if you don't want to, then—"

I hushed her with another chaste kiss, holding her chin in my grasp as he wrapped her arms around my waist, stretching on her tiptoes to try to press her lips harder to my own.

I almost laughed at her eagerness.

She was such an earnest girl.

I pulled away, and pressed a kiss to her forehead. "That is enough for now, empress," I smiled.

She gave a nod with a disappointed look on her pouting face.

I laughed, and I took her by the hand and led her back to my dragon, helping her up and riding back to the castle without saying much of anything else.

When we arrived, I watched her step over to her vanity and try to untangle her hair, but I grabbed the brush and started working on it myself.

"By the way, empress," I said, as a side thought. "You…are very pretty," I grinned at her in the mirror, and I watched her flush prettily with a blush as I chuckled, brushing out the tangles in her long white hair.

She was so easy to read.

I looked forward to watching her continue to grow.

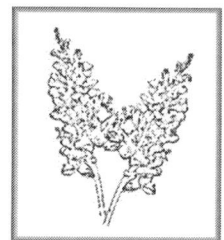

"But papa, I don't *want* her to start visiting me!"

"Conlaed," I said, tone stern. "*Please*."

"But I don't!" She pouted, looking out of the window.

It had been several days since my trip to the beach with the empress, and now it was back to my weekly visit with my princess. She was still making a fuss over being suspended, and she still had a month left to go.

I had decreed that starting for the last month, the empress would be coming on her own to visit the princess two times a week.

The empress had already agreed, in the name of bonding with the princess, and I hoped that my daughter wouldn't terrorize her too much.

My young bride was far too gentle and meek for her own good in this place, as my daughter would certainly not have any trouble taking control over the situation and trying to run all over my wife.

"I expect for you to behave, Conlaed. I am not joking. Your mother has been trying to get along with you, and you are being—"

"She is *not* my mother!" The princess burst. "She's just a spoiled princess from the north who got in the way of me and my papa!"

I groaned, rubbing my temples. "Conlaed…"

She noticed the change in my voice, and perked up. "P-papa," she said. "I don't want you to make me be nice to her. I don't want to be her friend."

"Conlaed, how do you think you will feel when *you* are sent off to marry one day?" I asked, and she startled, looking positively stricken.

"You…*you're going to send me away?*" She sobbed.

I looked at her, exasperated. "Don't you want to find a good husband one day and go live with him in a pretty castle?" I asked.

"No!" She cried, burrowing her face into my chest—hard—almost knocking the air from my lungs with her force. "I will never leave papa! I will be princess forever, before I become empress!"

"But you cannot become the empress of this nation," I told her, laughing. "You have to marry an emperor or take over an empire to become empress."

"Don't I inherit the title from you?" She asked, confused.

I shook my head. "*That*…is part of why the empress has come here," I said, already dreading telling her the truth. "Together…we will have a son, who will inherit the throne."

"But how come *I* can't inherit the title? I was born first!" She cried, upset.

"Girls do not succeed noble titles in our nation, princess," I told her. "You will understand, someday. You will marry a prince or high-ranked nobleman, and you will become his queen or duchess, or whichever."

"But papa!" She shouted, appalled. "You can't do this to me!"

"Princess—"

"No!" She shouted. "I won't go away so you can replace me with some prince that comes from that horrible ugly girl—"

"**Silence**!" I shouted, standing, and she flinched and started crying.

I took a deep breath, shaking my head. "You just cannot be reasoned with," I said. "If you don't want to marry, you don't have to…however, you still have plenty of time to think on that and consider it. You may feel differently when you get older. But you will not inherit the throne, and you will have a baby brother someday. You will learn, one way or another, what your role in this empire is. I have been far too lenient with you."

"Papa," she sobbed.

"The empress is going to start coming twice a week to spend time with you, and if I hear of you bullying her or being disrespectful, I have already planned out punishments for you."

"What if *she* bullies *me*?" She asked, an incredulous look on her face.

"She wouldn't do that," I said, waving it off.

She looked at me with an expression that told me to not bet on that, but I chose to not pay it any mind.

She was angry, and I was just going to make it worse if I continued arguing with her.

I stood, pressing a kiss to her forehead, and she pouted at me as I turned and left the room.

I strode through the halls to return to my room, and I gasped as I entered, finding my young bride standing on the balcony and staring at the dragons that flew in the sky above the beach.

I felt my heart tug.

Knowing she didn't have a companion, I felt sympathetic to her.

It must feel empty, to not have a drake companion to share your struggles and your feelings with. It was such an important bond.

For nobles in our world, who grew up learning from birth that at ten years old, they would earn their own companion to share their feelings and their lives with, who would never leave nor forsake nor betray them...? Then, to not have it, after all?

I couldn't even imagine it.

I stepped out there with her, and she smiled at me when she noticed my presence.

"The dragons are beautiful, aren't they?" I asked her.

I felt her body tense.

"I...I have something to confess," she said, and I felt my heart thump wildly at her statement.

Though we had gotten to be much closer and had become friendly, she hadn't gotten personal with me or opened up to me yet.

This could be an exceptionally important, life-altering moment for us...

"Go on," I said, hoping my tone was gentle. "I'm listening."

"Your majesty...your majesty, I don't have a drake companion. Not a wyvern, nor a—"

"I know," I told her, a smile in place on my face. "That is alright."

"What?" She gaped at me. She looked like she didn't believe me, and I could understand why she wouldn't. I was labeled as a blood-thirsty tyrant; a heartless monster who killed anyone that offended me.

However true that may be, I wasn't actually offended by her. "I said, I know."

"But...but aren't you *angry*?"

I smiled at her warmly. "I was at first. I was a bit angry about what that must have meant for you. I can't imagine how tough that must have been."

"But...don't you know what that really means?" She asked, looking at me with fearful eyes, before she plopped down in the chair nearby and dropped her face into her hands, forlorn. "I may as well not even be a princess."

"Look at me," I said, kneeling in front of her. She met my eyes, tears running down her cheeks. "I care about you, empress," I told her. "Whether you have powers or not, and whether you have a drake companion or not. You have been here for months already," I laughed. "Did you think I would suddenly hate you and send you away if you told me that?"

"Well..." She looked bashful.

I realized, with a sick, deep sinking feeling in my gut, that she had. She had really thought I'd send her away, or worse.

"That must have been very hard for you," I said. "You were brave to finally tell me yourself."

"So...you aren't going to kill me?"

I laughed. "I am a little offended that you think so lowly of me," I said. "I may be a tyrant, but have I done anything to you to give you the impression that I would hurt you because of that?"

She seemed to consider that, before shaking her head. "No, I suppose not."

I chuckled, bringing her into a brief hug before I pulled back to look at her again. "Then don't be afraid of me," I said. "And don't hide anything from me. This is your home, empress. *You are my wife*. Perhaps not in a romantic, physical sense yet, but you are my wife legally and in your position in society."

This seemed to make her feel a bit better, and she relaxed noticeably. "Thank you, your majesty."

"So," I said, walking back inside with her. "Have you decided what you're going to wear to go see Conlaed tomorrow?"

She looked at her wardrobe, opening it and showing me her clothes.

There was a small number she had brought with her, but I had brought in a tailor and had some clothes made for her shortly after she had come to the south.

"I'm not sure. I don't want to wear anything too flashy or luxurious, because I don't want the princess to think that I am bragging or being too extravagant. What do you think that I should wear?"

"Perhaps you are right," I said, thumbing through the selection and picking out one of the simpler ensembles. "I like this one," I said, appreciating the warm lilac color with white and maroon flowers emboldened on it. It was a high-collared dress with three-quarter length sleeves, tight fitted around the bust and waist but flowing out into a simple a-line for the gown.

She smiled. "Shall I try it on for you?" She asked.

I grinned. "Sure," I said, and we called the maid in to help her get changed.

I stepped behind the partition, but when I glanced up in the mirror, I flushed dark red when I saw her bare back...though, it wasn't purely a reaction to her naked flesh in a rousing kind of way.

On her back were several lingering, faded scars where the skin had been bruised and beaten but hadn't been treated.

It was damaged flesh, that was no longer bruised or fresh but was damaged.

Anger boiled my blood and I felt sick to my stomach, but I pushed it down quickly as I saw the dress fastened in the back, and I was directed to step back out.

I came back out, a smile that was warm in place. "That looks lovely on you," I told her, and I meant it.

The color stood out against her pale skin and her eyes popped against the bright maroon of the flowers.

"Then this is what I will wear," she said, smiling.

I could only hope that the princess would behave...in the meantime, I had some business to take care of with the North.

Once she had gone out of the room to go to the library with her escorts, I stayed behind and wrote a lengthy letter to the north.

Chapter 8 – Nieves

I took a deep breath, trying to calm my fraying nerves before I stepped inside the princess's bedroom to visit her.

This would be the first time that I had seen her since she had been suspended, and my first official visit to her without a banquet or tea party being the occasion.

I gripped my dress in my hands as I tried to ease my discomfort.

I wanted to get along with her, truly I did.

...Would she let me, though?

I could only imagine her being hateful and angry at me, and I was unsure about how to go about this without making her angrier.

I had heard that she liked the fire lilies that grew on the mountain, so I had requested the emperor the day before to send someone to go and pick some.

Much to my surprise, he had gone on dragon-back himself and picked a bouquet, bringing them back and letting me wrap the stems in a bright red ribbon to take to his daughter.

He gave me a hug of encouragement, and then I was off.

I nodded to the butler, and he directed me inside, opening the door and leading me in to find Princess Conlaed sitting there, sipping on tea and munching on her finger-sandwiches already. She glared at me, but did not speak.

The servants around us shifted uncomfortably, the air thick with tension.

I tried to remember my tutor's lessons on proper etiquette.

I gave a small bend at the waist and a slight dip. "Hello, princess Conlaed," I said, trying to be polite through my nervousness.

She didn't greet me.

In fact, she didn't make eye-contact with me at all.

I cleared my throat, my own body tension rising acutely, and I felt stiff as I sat down in the chair that the butler pulled out for me.

There was a nice, soothing warm black tea with milk and honey served today, as well as several choices of finger-sandwiches and other snack foods. There was even a tray of dessert options.

I gingerly took a sip of my tea, thankful that I wasn't assaulted by salty tea this time, and I enjoyed a couple of finger-sandwiches before I moved on to some sweet treats.

"Thank you for hosting me in your parlor, princess. The snacks are nice and this is a good tea," I smiled at her.

Again, she didn't look at me, but she *did* respond this time. "It was just what the servants decided to serve. I didn't have any input."

"Oh," I said. "Well, they chose well," I amended.

"You are wasting your time talking to me. I don't intend to be friends with you. Father has informed me of my role here, and I don't need some worthless, ugly girl only a few years older than me trying to pretend to be my new mother. I've never had a mother and I've been just fine without one. I don't *need* you, and I don't *want* you."

I didn't know how to respond to that, but I tried to smile through the spear of hurt that seared me.

It seemed like nobody would ever want me...

"I understand that you aren't fond of me, but I would really like to get along with you. I've been lonely, so it would be good to have someone to be close with here in my new home—"

"*This isn't your home!*" She snarled at me. "I will never be friends with you. If you're lonely, why don't you go back home to the north and out of my home?"

"Princess, I—"

"Don't bother speaking to me. You aren't wanted, here. My father made a mistake bringing you here."

"But, princess—"

"You are just a worthless, ugly girl who will never mean anything to my father. You wear ugly clothes and have ugly eyes and hair! My father will never love you, and I won't either."

"Well, I can't bl—"

"Did you know? Did you know that you were only brought here because he had no *choice* but to remarry?"

The servants murmured softly and stirred, restless, and I motioned the princess in a "hushing" gesture...but she just kept going.

"He had no choice because they were about to marry me off if *he* didn't choose a bride!"

"...Wh—?"

She didn't let me get a word in. "My amazing, loving, doting daddy...! That poor, poor man. He forced himself to choose someone, anyone at all, and he didn't want another girl from the fire empire because he didn't want to be reminded of my mother! He only agreed to have a new wife brought in to get her pregnant for an heir to the throne!"

I startled. I had somewhat known that, but to hear it so bluntly...so crudely...

"Princess..." I whispered.

"You shouldn't even be here," she seethed.

"I...I'm sorry—"

"He doesn't love you. He won't ever love you, and he told me himself that you are just here to give him a son! If you can't, I'm sure he'll send you away, and it'll just be me and him again! You won't last, so don't expect me to get close to you when you won't even be here for very long!"

"Princess—"

"You probably can't even give him a proper son, can you? He'd probably be as ugly as you, and what powers would he have? Northern ice powers or southern fire powers? I am sure that a boy with snow-kingdom powers wouldn't even be allowed to rule in the south! Any son you bear will be just as worthless as you!"

That was it. I'd had enough.

Just because I had been brought here as a womb for the emperor didn't mean that I should be treated this way.

My status was higher than hers. I was a princess by birth and an empress by marriage.

I would, one day, give birth to the Crowned Prince.

I didn't have to take this, did I?

"*Shut up!*" I cried, standing and shoving away from the table.

The princess, startled, backed up and fell over backwards in her chair, crying out as she tumbled to the floor.

As the servants rushed to help her on her feet, she glared up at me with a sharp, vengeful gaze and a wicked, spiteful sneer on her face.

An evil, giggling cackle began to resonate inside of her before tinkling out of her lips.

She threw her head back, really belting out a laugh.

"Just wait, you evil, vile girl! I will be sure my father hears of this, and you will regret the day you came to live in this palace! I will see your head on a spike on our walls!" She shrieked, laughing hysterically.

Fear penetrated the deepest part of my being as I felt the blood drain from my face.

I hadn't even done anything wrong.

I hadn't pushed her or harmed her in any way. She'd fallen all on her own.

I turned, dashing from the room, running as fast as I could in my long-trained dress through the halls.

I ran for the only place that I could think to hide that I was familiar with in this massive castle—*beneath my bed*.

This wasn't fair.

She seemed certain that I was going to be hurt for doing nothing...and maybe I would be.

I still didn't fully trust my tyrant emperor, after all.

Would this be how I would die?

I had been warned of one thing when I had come here;

that the princess was, absolutely, the greatest treasure of Kai Abeloth.

If she told her father that I'd bullied her, he likely wouldn't even give me a chance to speak, let alone defend myself.

I had to hide.

As the servants were rushing to the screams of the frantic princess in the room I had left, I bolted as fast as I could manage, and I dropped to crawl on my belly and crawl beneath my bed.

I got my breathing under control quickly, but tears rolled down my cheeks as I hugged my locket to me and clutched to my stuffed animal.

I was in big trouble. The more I thought about this, the worse it got.

The servants were not strong supporters for me yet—rather, they were quite neutral toward me at the moment.

If the princess ordered those servants from the room to keep quiet and then told the rest of the palace her version of what had just happened, I was sure that I would be beheaded for certain.

I was surely going to die for hurting his treasure.

I just didn't know what else I could do, at this point.

How could I ever get along with the princess when she resented me to the point of insulting me so thoroughly and directly, and now threatening me?

I knew that I wasn't her mother...but I was legally married to her father.

Shouldn't she be at least a little more respectful?

This was only our first private tea time, and she had already gotten me killed.

I didn't know why my fate hated me so, but I was obviously a horrible person in my previous life to have been destined to suffer this way.

I heard the door opened, and I lay my head on the floor that was starting to puddle with my tears, resigned to my fate.

"Where is the empress?" I heard my husband's voice ask in a shout, harsh and volatile.

I began to tremble even harder.

This was it. He was coming to kill me.

"Someone said that they saw her rush down this hall!"

"Hm," he said, stepping in.

I could see his feet beneath his bed through the other room, and he stepped closer to come into my part of our joined rooms and looked around.

I heard him take a deep breath, before he spoke again.

"Come out, *now*," he said, his tone cold. "There is no point in bothering to hide. You think I have trained in war to not be able to find a single girl in my palace? You were warned, I am sure of it; the repercussions for hurting my princess. Come out here and have some honor as the empress!" He shouted.

I gulped, thickly, my heart racing.

Should I?

Just face the imminent death with dignity, as he suggested?

This wasn't fair. I hadn't done anything wrong!

He stepped over to the bed, and I watched him kneel before his face came into view, expression dark...but his eyes widened as he took in my condition. "Why..."

My breath started coming out faster, and tears refreshed in my eyes as I began to sob, a pitiful, hopeless wail sounding through the small space beneath the bed.

"I...I didn't...I didn't!" I sobbed. My words quickly slurred together, unintelligible. "*I-want-to-befriend the princess but-she hates—*" I cut myself off. I tried again. In a voice rushed together and barely audible through my cries, I tried to explain. "I...I promise I didn't do anything to the princess, I just jumped up from my seat and she was startled by the table scooting toward her and fell backward and started threatening me and I ran because I was sure nobody would defend me so I—"

"Hold on, hold on," he said, setting down his sword onto the floor before reaching beneath the bed.

I flinched, and I felt his hands grip my arms as he pulled me out from beneath the bed. He pulled me into his lap.

"Take deep breaths," he instructed. "Slowly, in and out through your nose," he told me.

I started to follow his instructions, and I felt myself calming down.

"Good girl," he said. "Very good. Now. *Calmly*, from the beginning, tell me what happened."

I took a deep breath. "Well, I was upset so I stood up hard from the table and it pushed back toward her—"

"Empress," he interrupted, softly scolding. "You started from the end again. Start from the beginning. Start from entering her chambers."

I cleared my throat as he wiped my tears, and I took another deep breath.

I slowly told him what had been said, and when I told him what she had told him about bringing me in just to give him a son…I felt pain shoot through my heart at the guilty expression on his handsome face.

Then, I told him what she had said about the son I would give birth to, and his face grew very scary.

He looked over his shoulder to the maid, and told her to go and find the butler that had been servicing the tea time.

About ten minutes later, the butler and a maid stepped in with my maid.

"Tell me what happened. And if you value your lives, you will tell me the *truth*. Do not even delude yourselves into thinking you'd get out of this with just the princess backing you."

The butler and maid glanced at one another. "The princess...she said she would punish us if we spoke of—"

"And just *who* is *emperor* here?!" My husband snarled, startling me as he stood with me in his arms, setting me at his side on the floor, standing and gripping his sword in his hand. "Does the princess suddenly hold authority over the emperor himself?"

They both trembled and fell to their knees, but both of them finally began to recount what had really happened.

When their stories matched mine, he looked on in silence for a moment.

He took in the information, nodding in acknowledgement with a furious fire blazing in his eyes.

His face was almost...emotionless.

His eyes, however, burned and narrowed intensely as they gave their witness accounts, and he finally let out a long, almost hiss-like breath.

Finally, he turned to me and, truly shocking me, kneeled before me.

The servants in the room startled, falling to their faces.

"I am truly, from the bottom of my heart, *truly* sorry, my empress. My daughter has said unforgivable things to you. I will no longer insist on you trying to spend time with her, and I will not be offended or angry if you wish to have nothing to do with her in the future. She has shamed me as a father, greatly, with this shocking behavior. I heard her recounting and was ready to confront you for attacking her, but realize when I saw you cowering beneath your bed and crying...that you weren't guilty. If you had been guilty, you more than likely would have acted as if nothing was wrong. You were genuinely upset. I am so sorry."

I shook my head, clutching my fist above my heart. "I am the one to blame. I shouldn't have tried to talk to her at all. If I had quietly sat and had my tea, she probably wouldn't have been provoked."

"You should not have to sit in silence around my brat of a child," he grated out. "*You* are the *empress*. You have every right to sit and talk to her if you wish. I am beyond amazed by your patience and fortitude in dealing with my daughter," he said.

"But…"

"But?"

"Is…is what she said true? Am I really *only* here to give you a son? Did you only remarry so she wouldn't have to marry? Will I have to leave if I *can't* give you a son? Will you throw me away once I *do* give you a son?"

He sighed, running a hand over his face. "Please, ignore everything that child said to you. That was, *originally*, something that resulted in you being brought here; my need for an heir, I mean. That, and to protect my daughter from being married off. But no, that is not all that is not your only role or value here. And I wouldn't throw you out if you gave me a child, unless you did some horrible and unforgivable crime. I care about you. You have gone above and beyond my expectations and impressed me by how well you have handled things around here."

"So…do you…do you think you could maybe…love me, one day?"

He blushed, looking away and smiling softly.

His expression was tender. "Let us just say...that it is a strong possibility."

I blushed heavily. "Are you...angry with me?"

He stepped over to me and gave me a hug. "No," he said, and I heard his heartbeat beneath my ear, steady and strong. "Don't worry your head over anything, empress. You are safe. I am sorry I came in so angry. I hadn't been informed of the situation before I came to find you, I had only heard what princess Conlaed had to say because she rushed to find me and tell me."

"So...what will happen now?"

"Her suspension will be lengthened, and she is no longer allowed to host her friends or write letters. All of her privileges are being suspended, and she is being moved to the annex for a month outside of the palace. It is still on the property, but it is used as a guest residence usually when we have visiting royals or dignitaries. She will have none of her usual comforts for a while."

"I see...but your majesty, I..."

"Yes?"

"I object to that," I told him, and he gaped at me.

"What?" He asked, surprised. "But that is a light punishment, considering how she treated you. She even slandered our future child. I cannot let this go without consequence."

"I have a better idea."

Chapter 9 – Nieves

He seemed a bit perplexed, but gave a nod. "What is your idea, empress?"

"Lift her suspension and let her resume her usual benefits as princess."

"What?!" He asked, startled. "Empress, I don't—"

"Tell her that *I* was the one who lifted her suspension and disagreed with your punishment. Tell her what *your* plan had been. If she has her suspension lifted and her special benefits returned and is informed that it was because I allowed it versus what you had actually planned, she will be all the angrier about it and will likely contest that."

He gasped, shocked, but he suddenly became amused by this idea. "You are a bit wicked, my dear," he chuckled, dark, but he nuzzled my face with his own, and pulled back to laugh. "Alright. I will do so," he told me. He took a face towel and wiped my face, helping me pull myself together. "And you will come with me."

I gaped as he took me by the hand, leading me out and through the halls—passing shocked servants who were surprised to see me still alive—and we made our way back to the princess's chambers.

I hadn't anticipated that we'd be going back right away.

Though, I supposed that I should have, really. Every time that I had been affronted by some grievance, he had handled it immediately, right then. I guessed he would be doing the talking...

"Papa, you've returned!" She smiled and giggled, bouncing and looking happy and dandy, completely unharmed as he stepped in...that is, until I stepped out from behind him. "*You!*" She cried. "Papa, what is that witch doing here? She's the one who hurt me!" She sobbed, pouting her lips out and trying to give her father a terrified expression.

"Save your lies, Conlaed. I have already been informed of the truth. The empress's statements and the statements of all of the witnesses all lined up exactly, even when questioned separately."

"Wh-what?!" She cried. "Papa, they're lying—"

"Do you think I'm a fool, princess? Did you think that just because I am a tyrant, that I would fly off the handle and kill the empress just based on *accusation alone*?" He asked, incredulous. "She's a young girl not even five years older than you," he said, appalled. "*Of course*, I asked for her side and got witness accounts."

"Why couldn't you just believe me...?" She asked, genuinely crying now. "Why couldn't you believe your own daughter over a girl who's only been here a few months, papa? Is she more important to you than me, now? Is that it? Why?"

"Conlaed—"

"I guess I'm losing even more of my privileges, right?" She asked. "Am I going to be locked in the dungeon this time?"

"Watch your mouth," he said, turning cold. "If you *want* me to do that, I can. Actually, I had *planned* to take away all of your benefits as princess; take away your social gathers for quite some time, and send you to live in the annex on the property for a while...but, I decided to reinstate your benefits and lift your suspension, instead."

She stood there flinching and eyes tightly sealed for a moment, waiting for her punishment to be horrible...but then gaped at us with eyes that looked they'd pop out from her head when she heard that last part.

"W...what?" She asked, confused. "But I don't understand."

"You heard me."

"Papa..." She said, clasping her hands in a prayer hold. "Thank you, papa!" She cried.

"*I'm* not the one who deserves your gratitude, princess."

She froze on the spot, eyes wide and expression turning frigid as the blood drained from her face.

"...What?"

"*The empress* was the one who asked for me to lift your suspension and reinstate your benefits."

She gaped at me, horrified. "But...but why?" She asked. "I've...I...I don't get it!"

I gave a deep curtsy, bowing my head fully before I gave her a warm, as-motherly-as-possible smile. "I truly hope that we can become closer in the future, princess," I told her, and then I turned, walking away and back to my room as she sputtered and shouted behind me.

Just as I had predicted, she was much more horrified and angered by my kindness than by what her father had planned, and I could hear him chuckling beneath her spewing out angry words.

She was far angrier now than she had been before, and I delighted in the fact that this punishment actually upset her more than his would have.

...Perhaps he was rubbing off on me.

Should I be afraid?

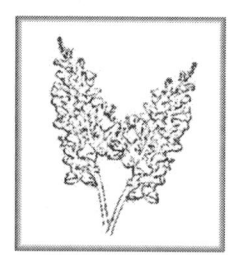

August, 722 FDD

As the months passed by, my tutoring really began to pick up. I was fully in the throes of learning my duties as empress now, and I had almost completely mastered the language of the fire empire.

My husband wasn't far behind in completely mastering my language, himself.

I had been allowed to take over management of the salaries of the servants and the taxes of the citizens, and I was even allowed to help oversee the salaries of the noble families.

As my birthday was approaching, however, I had been given something that I had no idea how to handle; *my birthday budget.*

The *former* empresses of the Fire Drake Dynasty had all planned extravagant, luxurious banquets and parties and shopping sprees for their birthdays…but I hadn't ever been shopping, and the only banquets I had ever been to weren't so lavish as all of that.

The fanciest I had been to, had been my own wedding banquet.

The emperor told me that this budget was gathered all through the year, and not to worry about the cost of anything; I was encouraged to spend as much as I wished.

I didn't have any experience spending such large quantities of money, however.

I wasn't even comfortable spending that kind of money…

It was then that I decided to do something different for my banquet.

I would find something that the princess liked, and we could do it together!

I began asking the staff, asking about what the princess usually liked to do, and I found out that there had been an opera she had been wanting to go and see.

I hadn't ever been to an opera, as the creative arts weren't highly expressed and weren't advantageous for the north, so I had no idea what to expect…but I decided to spend part of my budget to rent out the opera house for an entire day, doll myself and the princess up in our best clothes and makeup, and have ourselves escorted to the opera by the emperor himself.

That, followed by a nice, fancy meal, seemed like a wonderful idea to me.

I wrote out my plan in elaborate detail and gave it as a formal proposal to the emperor, stamped and laid on his desk with his other paperwork, for him to review…

Later that evening, he came to me with a very amused expression, holding the document and laughing softly at me.

"You were quite intent on making this a reality, so much so that you put in a formal request!" He laughed. "Alright. We will go to the opera. Are you sure that's something you want?"

I nodded. "Well, I've never been, and the servants mentioned that the princess loved the opera house and had been wanting to attend the latest concert. I thought it would be something nice to do together."

He gave a nod. "I am always impressed by your virtuous fortitude, my empress," he smiled, kissing the back of my hand. "Alright, we will go. I will rent out the best, top luxury spa that day for you both to be pampered and prepare, and then I will arrive to pick you up and take you to the opera house. Afterward, we will go to a fancy meal," he said. "Is that suitable for you?"

"Oh, yes, your majesty," I grinned at him, excited.

Several days passed, and it was finally the day to go.

The princess and I were led out to the carriage by our escorts, going to a fancy bath-house and spa for all kinds of skin and spirit treatments.

Nothing was said while we had our hair and nails done.

Not a word was spoken between us as we had manicures, pedicures, soaked in hot springs, and got suited for beautiful, formal ball gowns.

Nothing needed to be said.

We just enjoyed it in silence.

I could see, glancing at her when she wasn't looking, that she was actually having a good time.

She didn't want to admit it, but she was smiling and enjoying herself when she wasn't looking at me or close next to me.

I was just pleased to see her not upset with me for a while.

We finished getting dolled up by the artists, and a servant nearby alerted us that the emperor had arrived.

The princess was escorted out first, and I took one last look in the mirror at myself.

Did I really look okay?

I felt like a silly little girl playing dress up in her mommy's clothes…

I was turning thirteen, officially a teenager. I was *officially* of marriageable age, though most girls courted their betrothed for a year to three years before the *wedding* took place. Most men preferred their girls a little more…built for child-bearing.

I had been told by the maid attending me at the warehouse that I wasn't pretty, and that I likely wouldn't be able to get married because of my lack of powers, thus making me a dud and a useless waste of a noble title, but the emperor had never treated me in that way.

He had told me that I was pretty, and he looked at me like I was some rare, exotic thing. Which, to him, I supposed that I was. I looked so vastly different from the people of his nation that I could see why I was so eye-catching and attention-grabbing.

"You look beautiful, your majesty," the artists clasped their hands and smiled at me, looking on in delight. "His majesty will be pleased! Happy birthday!"

I smiled at their bit of encouragement and I took one last deep breath before I moved to the doors, letting the staff announce me to the emperor at the sound of the knock on the door and open them wide for me to exit the building.

His eyes caught on me right away, and went wide with his surprise as his mouth hung open a bit.

I blushed, feeling hot at the blatant stare, but he came back to himself right away and gave me a small, reserved bow at the waist.

"It is good to see you looking so refreshed, empress. You look beautiful."

I smiled, stepping down to him and letting him take my right arm in his free arm, leading me and his daughter both by the arm to the royal carriage and helping us up into the coach.

We rode off to the theater, and surely enough, he had reserved the entire building for us to enjoy the theater without a crowd.

The performers were thrilled and exhilarated to be performing for the emperor, the empress and the princess themselves, and the theater was decorated even more lavishly than I had imagined.

Whether that was because of our visit or not, I was unsure, but it left a lasting impression.

The show began, and I glanced to the princess, who was sitting excitedly on the edge of her seat, fists clenched as she watched the stage with anticipation while the singers began the performance, hanging on every word.

I startled slightly when, surprising me, the emperor took my hand in his own and I glanced to him to see him give me a warm smile.

I settled back in my seat, watching the stage.

The opera's story was about...

It was...

I froze, startled, as I realized that one of the singers wore a white wig, and had her face and neck painted white.

Was she...supposed to be *me*?

There was also someone dressed much like the emperor, and a girl dressed like the princess. Even their ages were somewhat close to our own.

The story played through getting the request for marriage from the emperor of the south and me being excited to get to go on a fabulous journey.

When we had arrived to the palace, it showed me and the emperor falling in love, the story portraying a happy marriage and as "I" grew up...it became more *romantic* in nature.

The emperor and I flew around on the back of his dragon, singing the praises of love and how it changes all things as he displayed his fire powers and I displayed my non-existent snow and ice powers through special effects, and how I had calmed his fury and turned him gentle and kind.

To end the song, it portrayed "me" bringing forth a son, and the emperor proclaiming him the heir because of his powerful gifts.

I felt my face sting with my blush, feeling like a fraud.

I didn't have powers.

I certainly wasn't the love of his life, and I hadn't changed him in any way.

He truly wasn't a horrible man to begin with.

The only character who hadn't been altered was the princess. She was a bit spoiled but loving towards and doted on by her father.

My character had been a modest, demure, well-educated lady who was powerful and exotic and useful to the emperor, while the emperor was portrayed as a horrible, murder-obsessed monster.

He, however, didn't seem to mind the portrayals presented through this performance.

Despite my ill feelings about the show's story, the songs and performance and effects were all quite exceptional, so I had very mixed feelings about it by the time it had reached its conclusion.

When it closed at the end, the cast took a bow and we cheered.

I noticed that the princess seemed to have a somewhat similar opinion that I had—she had enjoyed the singing and effects and the overall performance, but wasn't happy with the storyline.

As we left the theater, the emperor turned to me. "So, my birthday lady, what did you think of the show?"

I smiled. "I have never attended an opera, but I was pleased with the effects and the singing. *Overall*, I had a very nice time."

"*But...?*" He asked, waiting for me to voice my negative opinions.

"Are you kidding?" The princess whined. "I wanted to hear the latest performance that they had released, but *instead*, I got to listen to a sappy romance that I don't want to even think about!" She pouted, shaking her head. "The good singing and art and effects aside, the story was terrible."

He raised his eyebrows. "I was quite pleased," he said, soft, glancing at me. "Are you also dissatisfied with the storyline's plot?" He asked me.

"It...it wasn't what I had expected," I said at last. "I had also thought we would be watching the latest show released. I hadn't been expecting to see a show made about our...about...about *us*," I said, blushing.

He smiled. "You realize, though, that as my empress...soon, we will become much like the story portrayed."

I blushed harder, glancing away even as he chuckled.

"I can't believe what I'm hearing," the princess grumbled.

"Do you have any idea how lucky you are that you got to come with us, princess?" He suddenly asked, looking at her with an annoyed expression. "It is the empress's birthday, and she didn't *have* to choose a special event that she thought that you would enjoy. She treated you for a day of pampering and theater, and you are being most rude and ungrateful."

She sighed, soft. "I am sorry, papa."

"Well, let's get something to eat!" I grinned. "Princess...I am not very knowledgeable about the south's cuisines or popular places to dine, so would you mind choosing somewhere for us to eat?"

She gave me a sideways glance, rolling her eyes before she huffed. "Fine, let's go to the Crimson Dragon."

The emperor had looked like he would protest my request for her to suggest a place, before she gave her idea. Then, he seemed to reconsider and gave an approving nod.

"That is a good place to go eat, indeed, and it has been some time since I have eaten there. Actually...I had already reserved that restaurant," he laughed, sheepish. "I hadn't anticipated that you would pick the very place I had already chosen. Good instincts, princess," he complimented, and she blushed and soaked in the praise.

She was such a simple daughter, just begging for attention and doting from her father.

We got into the carriage and made our way to the restaurant, and I was very impressed when, a while later, we pulled up to a very large, fancy looking building. It was built almost like a castle, with strange curved rooftops and strange windows and doors that were shaped like circles.

Strangely, it felt almost reminiscent to the emperor's palace, but the roofs of the palace were a little less curved.

We stepped up the stairs and into the restaurant, and I was awed by the moody red lanterns that lit the area, the beautiful décor of bright, crimson-colored dragons with golden claws.

There were beautiful plants and luxurious paintings interspersed around the building, and even a large pond filled with beautiful, stunning koi fish and lily-pads in the center of the room, like a center-piece.

We were met by a beautiful young hostess and led to a table in front of a large, flat-topped sheet-stove, where a man in a chef's uniform awaited us.

"Welcome, welcome, your majesties and your highness!" He said, greeting us with a deep bow. "It is my utmost honor to cook for you today!" He said.

He fired up the stove, and began dicing and setting chunks of meat and vegetables and portions of rice to start sizzling on the flat-top.

We watched as he made a performance of the cooking, seasoning and divvied out the portions to us one by one.

We clapped and thanked him for his service before taking a bite, and my mouth exploded with flavors that I wasn't familiar with.

It was better that anything I'd had in years.

The chef was quite taken with us when we told him how pleased we were, excited to know that we approved of his cooking skills, and even the other cooks who had gathered around cheered and chanted about what a legend the chef would be for serving the royal family—and the royal family liking his food!

As the chef cleaned his cooking stove and began to cook special desserts, I turned to the emperor.

"Thank you, your majesty," I said, softly. "Thank you for this wonderful day. I have truly enjoyed it."

He smiled at me, and startled not only me but also his daughter, the knights who guarded us and all of the witnessing staff when he pressed a small, chaste, gentle kiss to my lips.

"Happy birthday, my empress," he said. "Congratulations on coming-of-age."

I blushed, my heart pounding hard and fast in my ears as he gave me a warm smile, and the rest of the staff watched on, speechless.

Soon, our desserts were ready and I enjoyed a nice, warm molten-chocolate cake with melting ice-cream on top.

It was delicious, and I found that this was my favorite of the desserts I had tried since I had arrived so far.

I was a big fan of chocolate, anyway.

Now that I thought about it, my emperor's skin was a dark, bronzing tan. Dark enough that he looked like a bronzy-brown.

He was my own personal chocolate, I thought with a heavy blush. *With a strawberry on top, that red hair of his.*

We made our way back to the palace, and as the princess snoozed against the wall of the carriage in the seat across from us, I rested against the emperor and started to drift in and out of sleep myself.

"You can rest," he said, smiling at me. "Go on, close your eyes. Let yourself drift off. I will return you to your bed when we arrive."

Encouraged by this and becoming relaxed, I did just that.

I roused, though, when I felt my body lifted and taken into the palace, the servants speaking in hushed tones around us as they mentioned a set of nightclothes for me.

Nightclothes!

Oh, no. I needed to change…but I was just so tired, so—

I almost shot awake when I felt a pair of silky sleep-pants slid around my suddenly bare feet and up my legs, beneath my skirt. My gown was suddenly being tugged off, and I found myself being re-dressed in a silky, soft top to sleep in, before I was laid back down and covered by my blankets.

"There, good girl," I heard the emperor whisper, soft. I almost trembled. "Good night, empress," he said. "Sweet dreams," was said by my ear before I felt a warm kiss to my forehead.

I heard him step away and slide into his bed just in the next room, the doors separating our spaces left open as per usual.

I could trust him. I really, really could.

He had the opportunity to touch me inappropriately. He had the chance to force himself on me or touch me while I slept, but he didn't. He merely changed my clothes so that I would be comfortable, and even that, he'd done in a fast, modest, efficient way before he had gone to his own bed.

I could trust this man who had restrained himself. Surely, I could.

I found myself more in love with him by the day, and I was absolutely terrified.

Terrified that at some point, he would come to his senses and abandon me for the useless girl that I was.

Chapter 10 – Kai

November, 724 Fire Drake Dynasty

It had already been over a year.

My empress, Nieves, was now fifteen.

I would be twenty-five in December.

We stood out in the gardens, watching the colorful leaves fall from their trees as the servants shucked the corn and prepared the other vegetables brought in from the harvest.

It was almost time for the annual harvest festival, and the entire city celebrated the closing of autumn and the arrival of winter.

The empress was doing her duty well, helping to direct the staff in an elegant and sophisticated manner, conducting herself gracefully.

She had really come a long way since she had come here, and it made my heart swell to think that my city—or that I—had any part of that.

Since her thirteenth birthday, she and the princess had been having two tea-times a week…though, limited progress had been made.

By progress, I meant only that the open hostility had ceased. The princess was no longer *openly* hostile towards the empress, though she did occasionally pull small, miniscule pranks on her.

The empress insisted she was unbothered by this, however.

They still didn't have conversations or talk much, and the princess wasn't on friendly terms with the empress, but at least she wasn't blatantly bullying or trying to get her into trouble with me, anymore.

I took the empress by the hand as she finished her duties in the garden as I often did, since she loved the gardens on the estate. The only thing I'd added since she had arrived had been a field of snapdragons—though, I hadn't actually shown it to her yet. It was going to be a surprise, once the flowers had time to grow and flourish. I had a feeling she'd be happy.

Snapdragons were her favorite flower, and it had been something that she'd missed since coming here.

She told me that she had a field of them back in the North in which she visited often, and that it was a place in which she spent a lot of time.

I led her through the halls to go to the princess's palace for her tea-time.

She smiled at me warmly as we walked hand in hand, and she took a deep breath of relief when we stepped into the warm air.

This autumn was particularly chilly this year...likely due to my furious letter of rage to the north two years earlier, when I threatened to cut off all trade after learning the truth about the princess that they had given me.

The king of the north had said that his sister must have done something absurd—tattling to me, when it wasn't even that big of a deal.

I had been so livid over how she had been treated and what I had found on her back, but the only response to that message that I had sent to him?

I had gotten was a *letter of regret* over failure to control the staff, and the sheet showing proof of termination of the maid who had been in charge of my bride during her stay in the North—which I had found out, later, had actually been a small, dilapidated warehouse on the edge of the estate.

When I had failed to send our shipment to the north for the trade and insisted that an apology was not enough to compensate for her suffering...the autumn had grown quite frigid, quite *quickly*.

Though, not much had changed over the two years since then.

In all likelihood, we would be going to war with the north soon...but I didn't tell my empress this news.

I wasn't sure how she would react. Would she be upset?

I tried to hide it from her as best that I could, because I didn't want to alarm her or make her feel guilty, as I knew she would if she knew a war might break out because I was fighting for her.

Still, I knew that I could win a war fairly easily, especially against the young northern king.

I had conquered many battles so far, and I was confident in my ability to make the young northern king bow at my empress's feet to seek forgiveness.

I glanced to my wife as she approached the butler, taking her in.

She was even more beautiful than she had been before.

She was a lovely, pale complexion. Her eyes were much happier, now, and she was more trusting.

She was warmer, in general.

The biggest thing of all that had impacted me the most, was...that *I truly enjoyed her being here.*

"It is getting cold out there," she said. "Do we have enough provisions for the winter for the castle and the citizens?" She asked the butler.

He started thumbing through his stack of paperwork, looking over the list. "There are several things that we need to replenish, but for the most part, we are prepared. We will try to make the right orders and get things restocked and refilled to distribute to the citizens," he replied.

"Thank you very much for your quick action and hard work," she smiled at him. "If you wouldn't mind, please bring some medicine for an upset stomach to the princess's chambers. My belly is a bit unsettled."

"Are you sure you shouldn't skip the tea-time?" I asked, and the butler waited to see if she would change her mind.

She shook her head. "No, no, I am fine to do tea-time. Afterwards, I will go and rest for the remainder of the day, though," she said, smiling.

He bowed with a warm smile to her, and I knew that I had made the right decision by handing over her duties to her when I had.

She was doing such a good job in her role.

When we entered the princess's bedroom, Conlaed—now eleven—had a somewhat...*suspicious* smile on her pretty face, but she beamed at me when she saw me.

"P-papa!" She said. "I-I didn't expect *you* for today's tea-time!" She said.

I smiled. I could already see what was happening here, but I decided to wait. "I wasn't going to stay. I just wanted to escort the empress here."

"I see," she said.

"*Conlaed*," I said, suspecting a trick. "What is going on? Why are you acting...nervous?"

"Nervous? I'm not nervous!" She laughed, but the sound was uncomfortable at best. "Please, sit down, step-mother," Conlaed said. "Let's get to tea."

The empress strode over to her upside-down tea-cup and lifted it quickly, noticing that—thankfully—there wasn't a toad under it this time.

That had been one of the princess's former tricks on her.

She took a sigh of relief, before she glanced over to the basket of sweet muffins. She lifted one, and took another breath of relief to find no spider.

Again, another of the princess's former pranks.

She tugged out her chair and sat down as I turned to leave, and I froze when I heard her gasp sharply.

"Step-mother, my goodness, what a *mess*! You should get that cleaned up!"

I spun back around to find my empress spinning to try to see what was on her bottom—and I felt my heart almost stop at the bright, striking stain of red on the bottom of her light-pink dress.

It *looked* like she had…menstruated on her gown.

I held my breath, wondering for an instant if *this* was the prank or not.

She *had* complained of her belly being unsettled, and it was well past the age for her to start monthly cycles, so I actually *wasn't* positive…

That is, until the princess started laughing and pointing, and held up a cup of sloshing red liquid.

"Ha! Fooled you, step-mother! It is just wine mixed with melted chocolate! You should have seen your—uh, um…step-mother, why…why are you—"

I strode over to the empress, shoving past the princess as tears ran down the empress's cheeks, and sobs started to silently break her breathing as she choked on them.

Rage fueled me, and I acted quickly.

I wrapped her up in my cloak, pulling her up into my arms in a princess' hold, and swiftly left the room after shooting the princess a glare and telling her that I would deal with her later.

As we strode through the halls, the servants looked on, baffled, as the butler caught up with us with a glass of water and a cup of medicine.

"Your majesties! Is something wrong? What has happened...?"

"My daughter played the cruelest prank so far," I snarled. "Station a guard at her door. She is not to leave her room for the rest of the week."

"R-right away, your majesty!"

The empress was barely holding herself together as she clutched tightly into my chest, her breathing ragged and harsh as she struggled.

I could only imagine how embarrassing and ashamed she felt.

When we reached our chambers, I sent the maids to prepare a new set of clothes and a bath for her as I helped her get undressed.

Finally, when the maids had left the room and it was just us, alone...she broke.

Her sobs finally had sound, and she began to wail forlornly.

"I am so sorry, empress," I said, stroking her hair. "I am so sorry that my daughter embarrassed you."

"I...I'm not *embarrassed*...I'm...I'm *upset*."

That wasn't what I had expected. I had figure that she was humiliated. Rather than that, upset?

"Tell me," I encouraged, rubbing her back in soothing strokes.

She took a deep breath. "The princess wouldn't have thought…of using *that*…as a prank…if I was normal and…and I had already started…having monthly cycles!" She cried. "I can't even…I can't be a true wife until I can have children," she sobbed.

"Ohh," I said, sorrow filling me as I saw it from a new perspective.

She wasn't just embarrassed because she looked like she'd had a cycle…she was *ashamed* because it *wasn't* actually real, and as an empress expected to conceive, carry and bear children, she *wanted* it to be.

"I don't…I don't know if I can stay here forever!" She cried. "What if you get angry at me when I'm older because I can't give you heirs!"

"Nieves, shh, shh…I would never kick you out for such a reason. There are other methods if you aren't able to, you'll see. I can adopt, or I can bring in a surrogate…I don't have to have my heir come from you if your body cannot do so. You need not feel ashamed."

"But…but you married me for heirs!"

I sighed, looking away. "But that isn't why I have stayed married to you."

She started to calm down, and I brought her into a hug. "R-really?"

I nodded. "That's right."

She sniffled, and I dried her tears as the butler came in and brought her the medicine.

"What…happened, if I may be so bold to ask?"

I sighed. "Conlaed thought it would be appropriate to make it look like the empress had started her monthly right then and there..." I groaned, shaking my head, and the butler and maid gasped, sympathetic expressions sent to my bride.

Of course, they knew from the laundry and from talking to her and myself, personally, that my young wife hadn't started her cycles yet.

They knew how big of an insult what the princess had pulled really was.

"I don't know if the princess meant it in such a cruel way or if she truly was trying to make a meaningless prank, but it wasn't appropriate and it wasn't okay," I said, taking my wife's face in my hands even as she continued to cry and bubble out small hiccups and pressed a kiss to her nose and cheeks, dotting her face with affection.

"Come, your majesty, we will get you changed and into the bath," the maid said, leading her into the bathroom.

I swiftly strode out of the room, back through the halls and to my office as I sent the butler to fetch the princess for me.

I'd had enough.

I sat there by the roaring fire, as my daughter was brought into my office, where she sat in a nearby chair and wringing her gown skirt.

"F-father...I didn't mean for it to make her cry. I didn't realize it would upset her—"

"Conlaed," I interrupted, and she piped down right away. "You will be twelve, soon, and you will have an entire new set of responsibilities and expectations fall onto you. Do you know that?"

"Yes, papa…"

"Do you understand what you did today?"

"I…I embarrassed the empress."

"You hurt her feelings," I snapped. "You didn't just embarrass her, Conlaed. You hurt her feelings. She is *still* crying."

"W…what?"

"Princess…what are you expected to do, when you are a woman?"

She flinched, and wrung her skirt harder. "I am expected to move to a new home, marry a high-ranked nobleman, and give him heirs."

"Do you know what is required for a woman in order to be able to make heirs?"

She hesitated, but gave a small nod. "You…must have monthly cycles of bleeding."

"Did you know that *most* noblewomen grow up with the impression and the line of thought being trained into them that, in order to hold any value, they must produce strong, healthy heirs for their husbands?"

She gave a slow nod. "Yes, papa."

"Do you understand why what you did is so bad? Do you know why it hurt her feelings, rather than just embarrassed her? Why she didn't shrug it off and laugh?"

She shook her head. "No, papa."

"Just before we went to your rooms, the empress was experiencing stomach pain. Then, when you pulled your stunt, she thought she had really started her cycles."

"But, why would—"

"She hasn't had a single cycle in all her life, Conlaed."

She froze, a stricken, blood-drained expression. "W...what?"

"It has been kept under wraps and hidden so that the advisors on the council don't try to replace her, but she still hasn't started her cycles. You didn't just embarrass her because she thought she had begun the cycle, you hurt her feelings when she realized that she *hadn't* and that it was just a prank."

Tears finally welled up in her eyes, and she finally seemed to understand.

"Oh...oh, *no*," she said, tears falling. "Papa, I...I didn't mean to...I didn't know..."

"*No more pranks*, Conlaed. I let it go while it was still innocent and she laughed it off and made it seem like no big deal, but you seriously hurt her feelings this time. I expect you to go and sincerely apologize, and then go back to your chambers. You are under probation for a week, with no visitors."

I expected a fuss, but she shocked me when she bowed her head. "Yes, papa." She stood, giving a curtsy, and stepped out of the office.

I sighed, slumping back in my seat and taking my head into one hand, rubbing my face.

Oh, that poor girl.

To have to get your hopes up for something so unpleasant like that, and then be disappointed when it wasn't real...

No woman looked forward to monthly bleeding.

I remembered my own mother, crying in bed with cramps and sweating and severe discomfort when she bled, but my father always perversely happy.

As soon as her bleeding was over...he was on her like a wild dog.

I remembered one time, when I was about to be ten, lightly stepping through the halls with a glass of water I had fetched during the night...only to hear strange sounds, suddenly. Curious, I peeked into my parents' bedrooms to see my mother on her belly, crying and groaning, taking quick and sharp breaths as she struggled to keep pillows out of her face and clutched the blankets...as my father beat his hips into her rear end and pulled sharply on her flesh, leaving welts on her tender skin.

They were naked and sweaty, and with a final thrust of force and a long, thickly satisfied sound, my mother sobbed and groaned into the bedding, gripping it until her fists turned white even as my father laughed and popped a loud slap on her bare bottom, making her flinch sharply as she sobbed into the bed.

As an adult looking back on the scene, I understood what it all meant, now.

My mother had mentioned to me, once, that she had loved someone before my father. He had been a knight, but he had died in the war that my father had started, and my father found my mother in the crowd mourning the fallen soldiers in a ceremony to honor their lives...and he took her to become his empress.

She hadn't been particularly willing, but he was the emperor and what he wanted, he got.

A few months after their marriage, and she was pregnant with me.

Then, just under two years after I had gained my powers when I was almost twelve, my father had perished in the same, still on-going war.

It hadn't been until I had gotten old enough, at the age of twelve, to go to the front and finish the war at the age of thirteen, that it had ended. Then, I had been wed to the empress and bedded and had a child nine months later.

It made me sad to know, now, that my mother had been taken against her will all of those years.

I resented my father for that. I felt, for a long time, that my mother couldn't have been too happy about my birth, considering the circumstances.

Though, she had never complained to me. She hadn't once told me that she blamed me. She had never conveyed anger towards me.

Before her death from sickness, she had been kind and compassionate and perfectly, affectionately motherly toward me.

I sighed, wondering how I could make the empress feel better.

I heard, later that evening, that the princess had gone and sincerely, genuinely apologized to the empress…though the empress had, surprisingly, numbly nodded silently and sent her away before going back to crying.

She was distraught.

I had to wonder when she would get better...and I also, respectively, had to wonder when she would start her cycles, if ever.

Chapter 11 – Kai

December, 724 Fire Drake Dynasty

It was the winter exchanging of gifts in the empire, which also happened to fall on the same day as my birthday.

My father had started the tradition when I had turned a year old, because he wanted everyone celebrating my birthday with him.

It was a time of celebration and giving and happiness, because I made him so happy, as his heir.

So, in honor of that custom, the royal family spent the entire day feasting and exchanging gifts.

This was my bride's first gift giving day, so I had prepared an extra special surprise for her; I was throwing a ball in her honor.

She had cheered up significantly shortly after the incident with the final prank the princess had pulled on her, and she had tried to move past it. At the annual physician's check-up, they insisted that she was healthy and that her body would start its cycles soon enough on its own.

That had seemed to comfort her a good bit, and she had started to perk up after that.

So, I thought a ball might be a good idea.

A day of pampering and getting dolled up, followed by a party and food and dancing.

It was about to be time for us to hold another ball again, anyway. As the emperor, we held multiple balls a year—or, we had, before I had become the emperor.

I didn't take that approach to my ruling, but I had thrown several banquets and balls in my years as emperor.

The last one we'd had was when the empress and I had married three years before.

Though we had married in December of 721 FDD, it had taken her several weeks to arrive, so she had celebrated the ceremony with me in January of this year.

It was crazy to me, how she had been here for almost three years already. We had already been through so much together.

The day passed, and we all congregated to the banquet hall that was now prepared and ready. I was announced with my daughter, and we were able to dance to a song before the empress was announced.

When she stepped in, I was in awe of how beautifully made-up she was.

She matched me, wearing a bright red dress emboldened with striking golden dragon patterns.

The neckline was cut as a high collar, but the center of the collar stood open, jutting down her chest in a slit, and there was bright golden fabric covering the would-be-exposed part of her chest.

It was tight fitting around her chest and waist, tight on her gently-curving hips, and a gentle a-line gown that was slit down the sides from her calves down.

The sleeves were sheer, shimmery red fabric that showed her arms through it.

Her face was touched up with a thin layer of powder, and a gentle pink lip-stain was coloring her lips. Her eyes were darkened by a soft, moody-red eye-shadow and her lashes were thickened with mascara.

"You…look absolutely stunning," I told her, giving a full, formal bow and taking her hand in mine, kissing the back of her hand.

She blushed, giving me a full curtsy and thanking me in her mother tongue.

"Ah, I see," I smiled. "You want to communicate this way, tonight?"

She nodded. "It will make the people think we are very close—"

"Thus, boosting your reputation and making us look better to the advisors," I said, liking her train of thought. If they thought that we were close, they would think that we were moving closer to an intimate relationship.

Which, we were…but slowly.

I took her hand, leading her onto the dance floor as we continued talking in her mother tongue.

"How have you been feeling lately? Have you still been feeling unsettled in your stomach?" I asked. "Should I dance slower?"

She smiled. "I am alright tonight, I took medicine before the ball. Thank you for your consideration, your majesty."

I smiled. "You have been here for almost a third year, now, but...we have been married three years next week," I told her.

Her eyes widened. "Already?"

I smiled at her again. "Yes, already. It is hard to believe, isn't it?"

She laughed as I dipped her. "Yes, it is. It feels like much longer. I feel like I've known you for so long..." She blushed.

I smiled. "We have been through a lot already," I said. "I...I am sorry, again, for how much Conlaed tortured you. It was excessive."

She looked away. "It is alright. She hasn't been that cruel to me since the last incident. She has even started to initiate light conversation, finally," she smiled.

"That is wonderful news," I said, spinning her and catching her when she almost lost her footing.

The song ended, and light applause sounded as we both blushed, before I led her over to the banquet table and got her a plate set in front of her.

"Thank you, your majesty, for how much you have done for me. You have been so much better to me than I had imagined when I found out where I was going. I was so afraid and nervous, but...you have been so warm and kind. Far better than I've ever deserved—"

I cut off her self-deprecating statement by pressing a light, chaste kiss to her lips, before I leaned down on her level to give her eye contact.

"Don't speak of yourself that way. You are a lovely young lady," I told her. "And I may have just chosen a random name at the beginning, but after I met you and we started getting to know one another...I realized how much I care for you, how I enjoy your presence here. I don't want you to go anywhere. I...I like having you here."

She blushed much darker, and we suddenly came back to reality as we noticed everyone staring at us, gaping openly at public display of affection.

We cleared our throats and blushed while stealing glances at one another, continuing our meal and letting the rest of the ball happen without much talking.

We were both a bit...over-sensitive and over-stimulated.

I hadn't ever had a real romance before, and though this might not have been the first time that I had kissed her, each time left my heart pounding hard and fast like it *was* the first.

I was a bit inexperienced, embarrassingly.

I'd always had a horrible reputation, so women hadn't often tried to work their way into my life.

As I took her hand and led my wife out of the ballroom, I noticed that she was stumbling just slightly. I lifted her into my arms swiftly, and she blushed heavily as I lifted the edge of her gown to see the backs of her heels rubbed raw.

"Empress," I scolded lightly. "You should have told me sooner, I would have let you get off of your feet," I said. "Come, let us go rest."

I carried her through the halls and to our chambers, where I asked a maid to get a large tin full of hot water and herbal salts to soak her feet.

I took off my wife's shoes as the maid scurried off, and I kneeled.

"Oh! Oh, goodness, your majesty, I—"

"Shh," I said, waving it off and lifting her foot to rest on my knee. I began to massage, and she blushed heavily as she flopped her head into her hands, covering her eyes.

"Ohhh," she moaned. "It feels…so nice," she said. "I didn't realize how much my feet hurt."

I chuckled, working over her feet and feeling her body start to relax.

The maid rushed back in with the tin of water and herbal salts, and I lifted her feet and set them into the warm water.

She took a deep, slow breath, and smiled at the maid, thanking her, before she turned to me again. "Thank you, your majesty. This is lovely."

"Of course. You are my empress," I told her.

After her feet had soaked for a while and she was starting to nod off into sleep, I lifted her and carried her to the bed, where I changed her clothes like I had in the past and covered her with her duvets, before I pressed a kiss to her forehead and stepped back to go to my own bed.

She shot out her arm, startling me before I looked back at her.

"I...stay," she whispered, glancing up at me drowsily. "Please...?"

I gasped softly, but she slid over a bit and I slid into the bed with her.

I watched as she finally succumbed to sleep...and I brought her into my arms, letting her rest in my hold as I slipped into slumber myself.

This felt different than it had with the former empress. When she had slept in the same bed as me, she had groped me and ran her hands along my nether regions almost constantly.

Her presence made me feel hot and uncomfortable.

However, my current empress was small and tender like a bunny in the embrace of a mighty wolf, and she was a calming and soothing presence in my arms. She clung to my shirt in her sleep in a soft, innocent manner.

She was on a level in my mind far greater than the former empress had ever been.

There wasn't even a comparison between the two.

How had I gotten so lucky?

I couldn't imagine it getting better than this.

I was finally falling...into something so, incredibly, delectably sweet.

February, 725 FDD

January had come and gone with a fabulous parade to celebrate the three-year anniversary of the empress's arrival and coronation, and we spent the day resting in the parlor reading books and enjoying hot chocolate by the fireplace while the empress and princess worked on their embroidery.

Now, it was officially time for the princess's coming-to-power, and I would be taking her and the empress, as well as the other highest-ranked nobles and advisors to the nation, to the top of the summit on the southern mountain for my daughter to get her powers and to meet her new dragon or griffon companion.

When we had attempted this ceremony back when my daughter had turned ten, the mother of my daughter's dragon had arrived, informing us that the chosen dragon soul born to my daughter was housed in one of her eggs, waiting to hatch.

It had started to glow, letting her know what was happening, but because it wasn't hatched yet, there was little to be done.

She asked us to wait for two more years; long enough for the dragon to hatch and learn to fly. We had agreed wholeheartedly.

Now, it had been the allotted time, and we were here at the summit yet again. My daughter had already started developing her abilities, but she was just waiting for her companion.

She dressed in a golden dress with red insignias of flames all over it, a red ribbon tying up her hair.

She looked ready.

My empress dressed in a simpler, soft red dress with golden patterns and a gold ribbon tying up her hair.

We climbed onto my dragon, and all of the nobles joining us flew up on their respective dragon and griffon companions to the summit with us.

There were drummers drumming, chanters chanting and humming, and I went to stand at the base, where a podium sat.

"Come forward, Princess Conlaed."

She stepped up to me, and we laced our hands as she stamped her hand in the red ink and left her hand print on the wall to mark her ascension, yet again. Her handprint covered her print from two years ago.

Cheers erupted as red and gold mist began to swirl around her, and I watched with pride as a bolt of flames shot down from the sky.

We all looked up to see a small, young dragon in a copper shade with red tips on its wings; a young female.

She flew over to us, landing in the center of the crowd and strutting rather arrogantly up to the princess, giving her a haughty expression.

She huffed, growling out in dragon speech.

My daughter spoke back, surprised to understand the dragon, and they communicated.

Then, the dragon shocked me when she opened her mouth and my daughter opened hers, and I saw a small string of electricity leave the dragon and enter my daughter.

So, she had the power of lightning, then, rather than fire.

The royal family usually had both; fire and lightning, as well as control over lava. However, women were generally quite a lot weaker, and it was common for women to only hold one or two of those abilities.

The dragon she had was of a weaker breed, obviously…but, I was immensely thankful that she wasn't like my bride, in that moment, as I glanced to my bride to see her looking positively…hopeless.

Hurt tugged my heart, and I remembered how hard it must have been, watching someone at one of these ceremonies when you hadn't even been able to have one yourself.

As the procession left, cheering and going to feast, I held back as I stayed with my wife, who was still standing at the podium.

"Are…are you alright, empress?" I asked her in her tongue.

She startled, but gave me a nod. "Yes. That was just a beautiful ceremony, your majesty. It makes me a bit sad for my lack of companion."

I gave her a sad smile. "Yes, I would imagine it so."

"Can I truly be the empress?" She asked. "If I don't have a drake companion, if I don't have monthly cycles…can I really be allowed to rule at your side?"

I had no answer but to hug her into my arms.

I had to find a way. I had to find a way to assure her, to help her. I needed to talk to my mages.

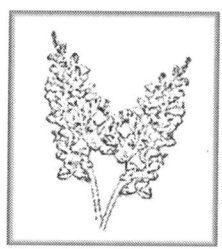

April, 725 FDD

Two months had passed since the coming-to-power ceremony for the princess, and I had remained consistently busy with my mages.

I studied my empress's bloodlines, studied her mother's and father's backgrounds as far as I could on the paper trail…

I was determined to bring her peace and reassure her that she could be my empress.

I knew, right away, that if she didn't start having cycles *soon*, the word would reach my advisors and she would be made to leave.

At best, they would change her title to that of a *queen*, and insist that I bring in a new empress entirely.

If they were feeling really generous, they may allow her to keep the empress title but bring in a new queen to give me heirs, and have my empress as just an honorary position.

They knew that I cared deeply for her.

In the three years that she had been here, it was a shock—to everyone who knew, anyway—that I hadn't bedded her yet.

The fact that I wanted to help her and keep her as my only wife said a lot, to begin with.

The mages had started to come up with a plan.

A potion that would gradually cause my empress to reach her puberty, and begin her cycles.

It was a move I hadn't wanted to make, but I selfishly wanted her to remain at my side.

I didn't want another empress, nor another wife.

"Give her a drop of this in her tea each morning and each night," my head-mage told me. "She should begin her cycles within a few months, at the longest. Hopefully, much sooner." he said.

I gave a nod. "Do not speak a word of this elsewhere," I reminded.

"Of course, your majesty."

I strode through the halls, making my way to the empress's chambers, where she sat reading a book.

She was so engrossed in the story that she didn't look up, so I took the chance to put a drop of the potion into her tea before I put the vial away and cleared my throat.

She looked up suddenly. "Yes, your majesty?" She asked, smiling. "I am sorry, I was so into the story—"

I waved it off. "Don't worry, it is fine. How are you feeling?"

"I feel well today," she smiled, and I felt my heart beat faster as I watched her take a sip of the tea, slowly sipping. "I am just enjoying resting, your majesty."

I smiled. "Good. You needed a break."

"I haven't seen you in a while. Are your many stacks of paperwork finally finished?" She asked with a laugh.

"Yes, indeed," I said. "I am sorry that I haven't had the time to spend with you lately."

"It is alright," she said. "I know you have been very busy."

My heart tugged painfully.

I had lied, telling her I had many stacks of forms to fill out and approve for the last couple of months, but I had really been working with the mages in my spare time.

I could only hope that I was doing the right thing…

August, 725 FDD

"Your majesty, have you bedded her majesty yet?" My head advisor asked, and I scowled at him. "You can give me that look if you wish, your majesty, but she is about to turn sixteen and you are coming to the age of twenty-six in six more months, your majesty. We are growing anxious, and news of war has been filtering in lately. As the master warmonger, we can only assume that you will participate, and we need a male heir, soon. Surely, you have bedded her?"

I shook my head. "I haven't."

"What?" He gaped, and the other advisors groaned, surprised and disappointed.

"She will be sixteen in three days," I told him. "She is still too young, she—"

"She is two years older than your grandmother when she gave birth to your father. She is only one year younger than your mother when she gave birth to you, your majesty. The former empress, the princess's mother, was actually quite old to give birth among the royalty," he said, shaking his head. "No wonder she hasn't conceived! *You haven't even bedded her.*" He sighed heavily, groaning. "Your majesty, you must bed her before the war starts in earnest."

"Then I still have about another year," I said, brushing it off.

"Your majesty!"

"*I am the emperor!*" I shouted, and they shrunk back from me, nervous. "How many battles have I fought? How much paperwork do I fill out? How many times have I bent to do what I have to, in my position?" I asked, exasperated.

"But your majesty—"

"I will make more of an effort to open up to her…but I am not going to bed her right now."

With that, I turned on my heel, stalking off to my office.

Chapter 12 – Nieves

"So…you think that I need to make a move on the emperor?" I asked the advisor, wringing my hands in my lap as I squirmed.

"The emperor, who is still a bit nervous about bedding a woman again, will *never* make a move first," he said, his tone genuinely sounding concerned. "I fear that his majesty will never make a move, and thus, your majesty, I feel that it would be best for *you* to initiate."

"But, wouldn't he dislike that?"

"I will be forward with you, your majesty…you will be sixteen tomorrow, and most of the former emperors were born from women younger than you…meaning that they had been bedded even younger than you. His majesty admitted to not bedding you yet. He is respectful of you, but part of his reluctance is out of nerves. To be frank, Empress Nieves…a war is brewing. If he doesn't have an heir secured by the time the war is in full earnest, and he goes off to fight…it would be devastating for our nation. At this point, the advisors are ready to bring in a secondary queen to assist the situation."

Fear spiked, and I felt my stomach lurch up into my throat even as my abdomen burned and churned.

I felt almost sick.

My back and belly were cramping, and I felt hot.

"I understand," I said, soft. I gave a nod. "I...will try."

"Good, then," he said, clapping a hand on my shoulder. "I know that you will not fail us," he said, walking out of the room with a bounce...almost as if he had won an intense negotiation.

Could I really do it? Could I really initiate the first move?

I didn't even know if I could manage to, in my current condition.

I had been cramping in my belly and feeling mood swings and hot flashes for weeks, now.

Though, the emperor always watched me with a small smile and hopeful eyes at our tea times and meal times...

Perhaps he was actually hoping for me, and was just too nervous to act on his own? I couldn't fathom any other reason he would watch me that way.

I tried to muster up my courage.

My birthday...!

My birthday could be a good occasion to try to get closer to him...

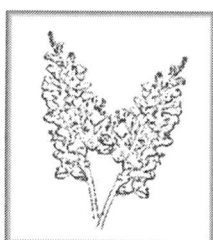

The night passed without much fuss, but the following morning, I awoke to a bouquet of flowers and a tray full of cakes and desserts—breakfast in bed.

I startled, looking up to see a bright smile on my handsome husband's face.

"Happy birthday, my empress," he said, tone rich and warm like hot butter, and it made my belly churn at the thought of what I intended to do later on this same day. "How are you feeling?"

"I...I would like to rest today," I said, smiling. "This is all so wonderful, thank you, your majesty," I said. I took a few bites, and then a sip of tea, before I felt him press a kiss to the back of my hand. "I am fine, honestly," I said. "I am just a bit tired and I am still cramping a little."

His eyes looked even more hopeful, for some reason, but then was masked by a happy grin. "Please, rest all that you need to, empress," he smiled. "I will be sure to let the staff know to be at your disposal. Eat and drink as much as you like. Whatever you wish, let us know."

"Thank you," I smiled. "You are so good to me, your majesty."

I would be sure to be good to him that night, I thought in my mind.

I wanted to make it perfect. So, when the emperor had gone, I turned to the maids.

"Please, bring me candles and flower petals, and prepare a bath enriched with special oils," I said.

They startled, glancing amongst themselves, before Ember looked at me. "Your majesty, do you mean...?"

"Yes," I said, nodding. "I am going to make the first move...tonight."

They all chattered quietly in an excited manner, anticipating their new duties to come.

For a woman to request the oil bath, petals and candles...it meant that she was preparing for intimacy.

Or, at least, that is how it worked in the South.

In the North, a man was always the one to initiate intimacy and set the night into motion. If he did not...then the wife would never be bedded.

In the North, it was highly frowned upon for a woman to initiate her own taking.

In the South, it was quite common. Women were so much more open about their bodies, their wants and needs and their desires than the women of the North.

I had been taught and well-versed in deflowering etiquette by my tutors, and I knew that the maids were aware that this was a very important step in our relationship that we had not yet taken.

Deflowering me would not only make me become a true woman, but also a true empress. So far, I had been an empress in title only. As soon as I was taken by his majesty, I would become the empress in body, as well.

I would command an entirely new level of power and respect, especially among the advisors and the staff.

Terror over the agonizing thoughts of not being able to provide an heir aside, at the very least, if I were already bedded, then I likely wouldn't be cast out of the palace entirely.

This was the best outcome for me.

I was led into the bath by a couple of maids, even as the connecting doors to my chambers and the emperor's chambers were closed, and a sign to not disturb was hung outside.

I was undressed and massaged all over with lotion to prepare me for the oils, loosening my skin a bit and making me even more supple, before I stepped into the hot water and soaked in the richness of the oily waters into my flesh.

I felt myself cramping even as my lowers throbbed in anticipation, imagining the emperor's body atop of my own as he became one with me. I hoped that I wouldn't be a disappointment…

My hair was washed as my body was massaged in the bath, and I felt a brush running through and taking out the knots.

Upon exiting, my body was left to air dry before I was wrapped in a sheer robe in golden tones.

My nails were clipped and filed, manicure and pedicure in progress even as my hair was trimmed and styled expertly.

I startled when I felt hands around my lowers, and I looked down to see them even trimming back the hair there—what little that there was, at least.

I gasped as I was spread open, checked to ensure that I was pure, and she nodded to the others.

"We will watch for your sheets, then," she said. "You will feel a tight pinch, and you will bleed…but this is natural, and you need not worry over it. It is the path to become a woman, your majesty."

I nodded. "Oh, I see," I said. "Alright, then."

"Would you like some snacks? An aphrodisiac?"

"I...I would like some snacks," I answered. "But no drugs, and no alcohol. I want to be completely sober minded."

They all smiled, and rushed to do my bidding.

Hours passed, and as the sun began to sink behind the mountains, I looked around the room one last time.

The candles were lit, incense burning and adding a thin smoke to the air. The incense that were burning were a stimulant that made you feel warm and fuzzy, and also numbed pain. It was specifically designed to take away the pain and nervousness of intimacy, while leaving the participants fully aware and sober. It smelled wonderful, amazing herbs that were highly sought after by many nobles and even whore houses.

Flower petals were littered on top of crisp, fresh white linens that would catch my pure-maiden's proof; my virginity.

I startled when I heard the emperor's chamber door open, and I rushed—quietly—to sit in the middle of the bed and the petals.

I heard a light knock. "Empress?" I heard outside of the joining doors. "Are you awake? I missed you at dinner, but I was told you were relaxing."

"Come in," I said, trying to sound normal and not panicked.

The doors opened, and when his gaze found me...I saw his jaw drop open, and a soft, gaspy sound leave him as his wide eyes slowly raked over the room before returning to me.

"Empress...?" He said, voice cracking softly. "What—?"

"I have prepared all of this," I said, trying to speak calmly. "I prepared this for you, your majesty, because there is something I want, you see."

He met my eyes, lips slightly parted as he took a step toward me.

"...And what is it, exactly, that my empress desires...?" He said, husky.

"I wish to have *you*." I smiled softly. "You have been so kind, so warm and good to me..."

He looked as if he had swallowed a frog, choking on held breath with eyes wide and a bead of sweat dripping down from his temple.

He watched on for a moment, before he seemed to come back to himself. "I will call for the servants to help you, my empress, to get you changed and ready for bed—"

"No!" I cried, too panicked. I calmed myself a bit. "No...I...I don't need their help, your majesty. I am in earnest, I...I want to truly be yours. There is no other way that I can be comfortable with your kindness, your majesty, without giving you *something* in return." I realized how ridiculous that sounded, suddenly. I scoffed, looking down at myself with my cheeks flaming in shame. "Not that I am worth much, as it were. I know that...Honestly, I know that I don't hold much value, that having me isn't at all of the same value as what you paid in exchange for receiving me in the first place. *I am not worth*—"

I was silenced by a sudden kiss on my lips, an urgent expression in his eyes as he cut off my self-degradation.

After a moment, he pulled away. "Were that so, I would never kiss you."

I sighed, looking away. "You only mean to console me, surely. You are kind, your majesty. I know you wish not to see me talk badly of myself. That would shame you as well, of course, as by being your wife, I am an extension of yourself, so insulting myself is the same as insulting your personal choice. I am sorry that I offended you. I see my mistake." I glanced at him. "Then…is it that you are not attracted to me? Do you not…desire me?"

He looked even further offended. "Of course, that isn't the case!" He said, firm.

"But how can I know that?" I asked, desperate. "You are kind, and you would say anything to console me, because you are fond of me. Why would someone as amazing as you desire someone lowly like me? I am probably more like a daughter to you. The others think so, too. I am too young, too childish to appeal to you—"

My self-degradation worked yet again, as I suddenly felt his hands tense on mine, moving and shifting to take my hips into his grasp and he was kissing me again.

This time, however…his tongue prodded at my lips, and I startled as his tongue gained easy access to my mouth, pushing and curling against my own.

Heat began to pool up in my belly, making me tighten and my heartbeat pick up a bit as I breathed hard through my nose.

His rapid breath in my ears, our eyes closed as we felt the sensations of one another…

I gasped as he pulled away, moving to kiss along my jaw and lower still.

His warmth spread through me as he kissed along my throat, along my collarbone and shoulders and spreading my sheer robe apart, taking my chest into his hands.

I cried out as he fondled me, and I felt my body shift so that I sat in his lap, straddling him.

When had I climbed atop of him…?

I felt something hard and twitching between my legs, and I moaned as he pressed it up and into me.

I vaguely understood what it was, what it meant…

He was turned on by me.

"This, my little empress…this is what *you* do to me," he husked out thickly, eyes half-lidded and heavy with desire as he gazed up at me. "You may do as you wish with me…but I am not above admitting that I am not very experienced. My…" He choked up, and I felt my heart tug painfully. "My only experience, I was tied up for the duration and I had no control. I don't know…"

"Your majesty—"

"Kai," he interrupted suddenly. He brought his hand up to cup my cheek. "When we are alone, address me by name. You have been my wife for over three years, and yet you insist on being formal, even still…"

I felt my heart clench, and my belly flopped inside of me, my heart racing as I gave a timid nod.

"Kai," I said, soft, as I took his hand in my own and led it to my hip. "Please…take the lead. Just…do what feels right. I don't have any experience at all, so I…don't know what to do."

He blushed, deep and rosy beneath the tan of his skin, but he gave me a nod and flipped us so that he rested between my legs, me on my back beneath him.

I felt my heart pick up again as he moved to kiss me, his hands roaming over me as I tugged and pulled at his flesh, too.

Gasping and trembling, we managed to undress one another and soon enough, he was looking down at me as he gripped between his legs, and I felt something pushing against me.

"Are you...*sure* that you want this?" He asked, and my heart throbbed at his consideration. "This is your last chance to stop, before..."

I gave a nod. "I want you, Kai."

He swallowed thickly, and he pressed as kiss to my lips, letting it get heated before I suddenly felt a slow, vast spreading and stretching, and then a sharp pinch as his hips slapped against me.

I cried into his mouth, and he held still even as he trembled in my arms while I dug my nails into his shoulders, trembling and whimpering into him.

He pulled back, looking down at me with a strained expression. "Are you alright...?" He asked, breathless.

I couldn't answer right away, instead nudging my face into his chest muscles.

I vaguely heard him shushing me, whispering how sorry he was for hurting me while I cried into him, even as I felt him twitching and throbbing inside of my body.

He was being so patient, so kind...

I hadn't expected for him to be so long-suffering for me.

I took a deep breath, wriggling a bit to test it out, and he groaned.

"I think that I will be alright…if you move, now," I whispered.

He nodded silently, a numb expression in place as he gave a few small, minor thrusts.

After a few more minutes of this, I felt myself loosening my death grip on his shoulders and I felt myself not hurting as much.

I gasped as his strokes lengthened a little, more fluid and slower, calmly causing friction within me.

I groaned as I felt him pulsing in me, and I clenched on him.

"You can move harder," I said, gasping. "I…I like it, it feels good now. I like it…"

I felt him harden in me, seemingly hearing what he had needed to hear, and his thrusts strengthened as he gradually increased the pace as well.

I felt something building as he pulled back, body straight as he pulled my legs up to rest on his shoulders, and he reached a hand to sit against my opening and I almost shot out of the bed when I felt him stroke something…something incredible, and absurdly sensitive.

I felt something building quickly, a heat rising in me as he stroked my insides over and over, all while his fingers worked over the sensitive nerves there.

"You are so stunning, Nieves," he whispered, and I suddenly throbbed and thrashed as I tightened, something breaking in me.

Heat flamed in my cheeks at my wanton sounds, embarrassed at my loud noises and the height of my cries.

He held my legs still with a soft, proud smile while I fell apart for him, gasping out as my chest heaved in the air with my heavy breaths.

"Good," he said. "I was able to help you reach it. That's very important," he smiled at me, before he spread my legs again and rested his chest against my own, kissing me as he thrusted harder.

Then, he suddenly paused, and he moved me to my hands and knees even as he propped my lower body up on pillows, and he spread my legs as far as they could go apart before he situated between them and thrust into me from behind.

I wasn't having to do any work in this position, propped up as I was, but he was suddenly so deep and so thick that I cried out all the louder, feeling the build up again as his hands massaged my back.

"Do you...feel good...?" He asked, a soft pleading in his voice.

I didn't know why he was so worried, what with how I was pushing back into him and loving the feeling, but he seemed to suddenly need this assurance.

"Yes!" I sobbed. "It is so good that I feel like I will lose my mind!" I cried. "Kai! Kai, I...I love it. I love *you*, Kai--!"

I startled with the force of his suddenly powerful thrust where he paused, fully encased in me as I felt him thicken and suddenly, he cried out softly and threw his head back when I felt warm and wet and full...

I gasped and trembled even as he pulsated within me, and I felt him trembling as he leaned over me, seemingly spent for a moment.

The throbbing...was delicious.

He waited a moment as he poured kisses and whispers of love on my bare shoulders and back, before he pulled the pillows out from beneath me. He helped me move to my back as he pulled me into his embrace, and I fell asleep in his arms quickly.

His still-rapid heartbeat beneath my ear soothed me, and I felt my fears drift off for now, satisfied that I finally belonged to him.

I had already been here for over three years. We had grown to be quite close in that time, and it felt all the righter that I had finally given myself to him this way.

I couldn't have felt more peaceful, in that moment, as I fell into a deep slumber against him.

When I awoke the next morning, I gasped and opened my eyes to find Kai lying there, facing me.

The sun beamed in through the sheer curtains around my bed, and stray spots of light lit the fiery tones of his hair, the thick darkness of his lashes that brushed his high cheekbones.

He breathed evenly, his muscular frame rising and falling with his breaths.

His thick lips slightly parted, I could hear his heavy breath as he slept peacefully.

I went to move and suddenly flinched in pain, and a moan escaped my lips.

I saw his lashes flutter as bright, burnt orange eyes with flecks of gold and a pit of ruby-red around the pupil opened, observing me.

"Are you feeling alright, Nieves?" He asked, reaching up a warm hand to stroke my cheek.

I nodded. "I am sore, and a bit thirsty," I admitted. "But otherwise, I...feel euphoric...Kai..." I smiled at him, and he sat up, pressing a gentle kiss to my nose before he stood.

I blushed heavily as his naked body left the bed in all of its hot glory, taut muscles and thick arms and legs with a tight, well-rounded bottom that was perfect for looking at...

He was the picture of masculine beauty, almost like a peacock?

No...

No, more like a proud lion, with a mane so fine that no lioness could resist him.

Women would fall at his feet to see him the way that I was seeing him now.

He strode into my bathroom, and I heard the water running and filling the tub. After a few minutes, he came back to me and lifted my body into his arms—albeit, I did protest a bit, but he ignored me.

He carried me to the tub, setting my body into the warm water and my aches began to feel better as the heat soothed me.

He went back to the room, and I heard him talking softly with one of the servants. Then, more voices from the maids entered, and within a few moments, he had returned to me, and stepped into the large tub himself, sitting across from me.

"I gave the sheets to the maid," he mentioned off-handedly. "With this, the counsel will know that you have been bedded as well. It is tradition in the South for the emperor to display the stained sheets on the palace wall. The whole of the women in this empire will hate you for a while, I imagine," he chuckled softly.

I startled when he lifted my foot, working over it in his hands, and I blushed as I watched his eyes rake over me like a carnivore watching its dinner.

"Kai..." I whispered. "I...I want you to know that I will try very hard to be a good wife. I know I may not be able to do everything that a wife should, but I will try."

"Nieves," he said, voice warm. "You know, you constantly surprise me." He smiled at me. "But you're already a good wife. Just focus on being happy with me," he smiled.

We sat just smiling, warm glances at one another and happy feelings radiating between us. It was a good moment.

When we had bathed and soaked a while, Kai lifted me to the side of the tub, drying me off with a fluffy towel and dressing me in a warm, plushy robe. He lifted me and carried me back to bed, and I was shocked to see the bed remade and done with beautiful, plushy blankets.

"I told the maids to be sure you would feel the utmost comfort, after…you know, last night," he said, a blush on his cheeks. "You should rest today, and relax. I will take care of you," he smiled at me, pressing a kiss to my cheek.

I smiled at him, feeling feelings bubbling over. "I love you," I whispered.

Startled, his eyes wide as he gazed into mine at my confession. "I…I thought I had misheard you last night, or that you had simply said it in the moment of our passion…" His cheeks darkened considerably, and his ears turned red. "You have given me new hope, my empress," he smiled at me, pressing a chaste kiss to my lips. "I care for you deeply. Though, I may not know what love in a romantic sense is, you are teaching me. I feel things that I have never felt before. I will let you at least know that you hold a large place in my heart."

"That is all I ever could have hoped for," I smiled.

In truth, I hadn't ever dreamed of that much, even.

When I had found out that I was coming to the South, I dared not hope for love.

For him to admit that I held a space in his heart was something that made my heart pound in my chest.

The day passed on with my husband catering to my needs, feeding me and making sure I stayed hydrated while I lounged around in bed.

Truthfully, I had started cramping and feeling sharp pains in my lower belly, and I wasn't entirely sure what they were coming from. I hadn't had such intense pain before, but I vaguely wondered it was because I had lost my virginity.

It was late into the night when I awoke with sharp, stabbing pains and a sudden gush of heated liquid between my legs that I cried out, terrified.

Kai had awoken right away, worried and concerned to see me curled in fetal position in bed, clenching my stomach. Then, he saw it, and a large grin passed over his face.

What on earth about my pain could cause him so much joy?

Fearful hurt spread through my heart, until the maids rushed in and gave the same reaction.

"What is everyone so joyous about?" I sobbed. "Is it nice to see me in pain? Am I dying?"

"No, your majesty!" Ember said, smiling and taking my hands in hers. "You have started your monthly flow—you have blossomed into a full woman in just forty-eight hours!"

I startled, and I looked down at the nice plushy blankets that I had been lying on to see a large, dark red pool of blood beneath my rear end.

Tears sprung to my eyes as the physician nodded, a grin in place on his face as well.

"Congratulations, empress. You have started your courses."

This...this meant that I could be a true wife, and a true empress...! I could give Kai an heir, I could—

I could get pregnant...

I could bear him a child!

Even as we cracked open some wine and the maids brought me a tray of sweets while my husband took me yet again to the bath to clean myself, I began to pray.

I began to pray for a miracle. I began to pray for a child.

Chapter 13 – Kai

January, 726 Fire Drake Dynasty

"H-harder! *Harder*, Kai!" She cried out her demand of me, clinging onto my neck all the harder and digging her nails into my shoulders. "It is so good," she sobbed, punctuated by my thrusts.

I held her up against the wall, my hips slapping her sweaty flesh as I stroked upward into her body.

She gasped and shivered against me, kissing me all the while.

Her breaths were heavy in the air, and I groaned as I felt her clench on me.

It was our four-year anniversary of her taking vows with me and becoming the empress, and since her sixteenth birthday, we had taken to making love.

A lot of love.

Often.

As much as we could.

Since she had given me my control back, I found that I wanted the intimacy as often as she would allow it, and I delighted in her warmth and softness. I craved it.

How I had kept myself so deprived until now, I was unsure, but once I'd had a taste, just once would never be enough.

I had to have her as much and in as many ways as possible.

We had already marked my office with places that I had taken her; on my desk, pressed against the wall, pressed against the window, held up with her gripping the bookshelf…

We had left our traces in the bathroom, both hers and my chambers, in the horse stables.

Even in the banquet hall on the dining table—I had let the servants know, afterward, to change the table linens…though, the idea of my staff eating at the same table that I had taken my empress on left me feeling giddy and giggly, like some naughty child who had been caught stealing from the cookie jar but still continued eating for the thrill of being known.

We had even made love in the future nursery for our future child, which had once been my chambers.

I had moved into her chambers, since she had wanted to stay in the room with the balcony for safety reasons.

I had taken her as she held on to the crib, braced against it as I pounded into her from behind while her breasts bounced in the cool air.

Tonight, I had started on a plushy blanket by the fireplace, but we had moved to multiple spots around the room.

"When it gets warm again, I…I want…"

"What do you want, Nieves?" I asked, full of anticipation.

This was a common game—a game in which she told me, in detail, all of the places and positions she wanted me to have her in.

"I want you to take me out on the sand. I want you to take me beneath the stars, even in the edge of the waters, and let the waves kiss against us as you thrust into me," she groaned, and I gasped as I suddenly felt it coming.

I slapped against her one last time, deep, pushing in as far as I could go as she cried out when I emptied myself into her.

I wondered, vaguely, when—*if*—she would get pregnant.

We hadn't gone many days without love-making since our consummation, but she still had yet to conceive.

Every month, I watched in horror as she broke down crying when her menses arrived, sobbing and gripping her knees as she felt like a failure.

It was hard to keep her confidence up, and I did my best to make sure she knew that I wasn't pushing her to get pregnant.

Though, I knew that the council was beginning to get restless, as well.

War was brewing, and it was already being discussed that other nations had already been biding for my favor in the war. They knew that I would be the deciding factor.

It didn't help that the North, my bride's homeland, expected me to fight by their side because I had married their princess. I had "familial obligations", it seemed, and they were already angry that I hadn't declared my intent to join allegiance with them as soon as they decided to enter the war.

The council was on edge, knowing that it had already been five months since I had started intimate relations with the empress, and she had yet to become pregnant.

I wasn't actually in a rush, but they pushed me so hard…

As the emperor, with a deceased father and mother and no siblings, it was certainly a nerve-wracking thing to consider; the young emperor going to war when he had yet to secure an heir.

Say that I happened to die in battle...my empress and the princess would face assassination attempts, marriage requests would come pouring in pushing them both to marry so that the men could assume my place as the emperor...

The council may even push them out entirely and replace my line, if they wanted to.

Without the dowager empress, who had even more say than the emperor in many cases, there was nothing that could be done.

If I lost in battle, without an heir secured for the throne...it would become complete chaos.

Mostly because my empress was not a conqueror herself, and was a complete pushover.

Had she been of a tyrant nature herself, I wouldn't have been worried. She could have the ability to become a tyrannical empress and begin bringing in a formal consort as well as concubines, and basically rule the nation herself, if she had such a disposition. However, my young empress was weak and timid, and I knew she would never do such a thing.

I understood why my council members were so concerned. They actually cared about me and my empress—at least, most of them genuinely did. However, some of the harder, harsher members didn't care.

It was imperative that I secured an heir if I wished for my empress to remain in her position, at least.

A few days passed by, and yet again, my empress wallowed in sorrow and hurt when her course came. I didn't know how I could comfort her, knowing how upset she was and how disappointed she felt.

Earlier in the day, I had received a full plea; a request to join the North in earnest against the west and central kingdoms.

I, however, did not wish to join the north.

I had a couple of reasons for this.

My brother-in-law full out *expected* it of me, firstly of all.

Secondly, with the rumors I had heard of how their people had treated my empress after she had been deemed powerless...?

No.

No, I didn't think joining the north would suit my wishes in the slightest.

However, I didn't want to join the west and central kingdoms, either.

What was I to do, then?

"Why not join the east, then?" My head mage asked. He shrugged. "They have been close trading partners, as well as strong competition against the North for so long, and even speak the same language. However, they have decided to stand against the west and central kingdoms *without* joining the north. You would be striking a blow against the north while not joining the west and central kingdoms, as well."

I contemplated this option.

"The water kingdom is rather similar to the north, but offer much more value in my opinion," my head advisor commented. "Joining them would be a good plan."

"And, should anything happen, the empress could take refuge there. Since they are of similar backgrounds and speak the same language, she would feel at home there, and having her there as a refugee would further hurt the North, if it came to that."

Well...I doubted that she'd feel at home, but she wouldn't be in danger there, in any case.

I nodded. "Send out a declaration, then. The Fire-Dragon kingdom of the South refuses to join the Snow-Wyvern kingdom to the North. The Fire-Dragon kingdom of the South *also* refuses to join the Earth-Drake kingdom of the West, and the Air-Ying-Long kingdom of the Central region. The Fire-Dragon kingdom of the South will join forces with the Water-Sea-Serpent kingdom of the East."

"I will do so at once," they said, and rushed off to do my bidding.

"You have made a choice..." My empress whispered, and I startled to find her walking into my office.

I sighed. I supposed that I couldn't actually keep this from her forever. So, I nodded. "Yes."

"You..." She hesitated, looking like she didn't know what to say. "You didn't choose the North..."

I swallowed thickly. "Does that bother you?"

She shook her head. "No," she said. "But won't that cause problems for you? My brother, he...he expected you to join him, because you have me, didn't he? He expects that."

"So what?" I asked, shrugging as I bit into an apple. "Your brother is a young king with no war experience beneath his belt. But there is another reason, too. They didn't treat you well, Nieves. There were mere *servants* who abused you and you were locked in a shabby warehouse on the estate, away from love and warmth and care. You deserved better. Why would I support them?"

She looked away. She hated that I had found out about that, and still felt uncomfortable talking in depth about it. Still, it was bound to come out sooner or later.

I had been appalled, originally, when she had thought I'd kill her for deceiving me about it.

"But the East...?" She asked, smiling.

"Have you ever been?" I asked.

She shook her head. "No, but we had several occasions of dealings with them. We were trading partners, but also competition. Water and Snow are basically the same. Originally, water came first. We actually broke off from the water kingdom when we discovered our powers for snow and ice."

"Yes," I said. "I had remembered that from my history lessons. They constantly fight each other over who is better and it is always in the spirit of competition."

"I met their prince, once. Sometime before I had come to the age of power, my father had mentioned that I may be matched with him one day. I didn't think that he ever caught wind of that, as my father was simply mulling over the idea...truthfully, once my lack of powers was found out and I didn't become the true princess I had been expected to be, he shut me away and I don't think he ever anticipated that I would have a chance to marry. They likely wanted to keep me locked away forever."

I took her into my arms, stroking her hair.

I couldn't imagine a life without her in it, anymore.

Thinking that her father had thought to marry her to the prince of the East, but then taking her chances of marriage away just because of her lack of power…it was hard.

Why did I feel this way…?

I was happy she hadn't married the water prince, but to know that the choice was taken from her just because of *that?*

It angered me toward the north all the more. What a conflict of interests…

April, 726 FDD

"Do you like that?" I asked her in a low, husky tone, thrusting in from above her as the waves lapped at her side as they reached us before pulling back out to the sea.

Just as she had wished, I had brought her out to the ocean, taking her in the edge of the surf in the bright, blinding light of the setting sun.

Her eyes tightly closed, mouth agape as she gasped and sucked in for breath, but her body trembled as I traced the outer edges of her breasts even as the water pushed against her again.

The water lapping at her sides and curves added so much extra sensation and stimulus that she was basically on the edge of cumming for a while, now.

"Ohh…."

I felt her getting tighter, and I moved us so that her rear was pressed against my thighs, legs straight out straddling my hips, and I spread her legs apart as I shoved my way in to the hilt of her.

She thrashed and cried as she broke around me, throbbing and pulsing over me and sobbing as her release hit her.

To feel her quivering flutters over me and tightening, clenching on my cock…it was utter bliss.

Exhausted, she relaxed her body as I lifted her, like a wet noodle almost, and I carried her to where I was standing hip deep in the water.

I turned so that the waves were pushing against my back, and I held her against me as I pulled out, not thrusting back into her until the waves thrust into my back.

I took her in time to the waves against me, and she clawed at my back and sobbed brokenly into my chest as I hit this new angle in her, with my cock angled upward into her cervix.

I lowered her, setting her on her feet and faced her away from me as I bent her slightly forward, and I gripped her biceps in my hands as I pushed into her with the push of another wave.

She cried softly as I moaned, thrusting again and again.

"Kai—Kai, I'm—"

Her voice cracked and I felt her pulsing and clenching on me again.

The sun behind me illuminated the clouds above us, the reflected light shining off of the sweat of her back.

I brought myself to bend over her, still stroking her insides as I tightened my arms around her and brought her up straight again.

I felt her bottom slap against my hips as I pushed into her desperately, seeking my release now.

"Nieves," I whispered hoarsely, and I felt myself swelling. "Tell me you're mine. Tell me that you belong to me."

"I-I'm yours! Oh, sweet merciful heavens! I belong to you, Kai!" She sobbed brokenly. "I'm *yours*! I can't imagine not being yours!"

I gasped, letting out a cry as I emptied into her, my arm wrapped around her shoulders and my left hand cupping a breast.

As I felt her clenching and thrashing once more, I pulled her head to the side and bit the junction of her neck and shoulder, sucking and nipping her flesh.

I felt her quiver over me, her body struggling to catch her breath as we both came down from our highs.

I lifted her in my arms, carrying her out of the water and setting her on a blanket I'd set up further up on the beach.

My dragon watched us casually, waiting for us to be finished and ready to go back to the castle.

Though the idea had made her uncomfortable at first, I assured her that he wasn't particularly caring about our lovemaking and was rather focusing more on protecting us in our intimate moment…

Not that I gave a fuck who saw us, honestly. I was the emperor.

I'd fuck my empress whenever and wherever I wished to, and not be a damn bit bothered if anyone was perturbed.

I'd already taken her all over the palace at any given time of day as it were. I didn't see any harm in my dragon seeing it.

Though, he had admitted to me himself that he was intrigued with the concept of mating for us humans.

Dragons were more like serpents; they performed a dance, before they got the body parts aligned and tangled their genitals together and released the sperm into the female. It was not so much in the manner of which humans performed.

He also admitted, too, that he coveted her along with me.

As my bonded dragon, he was attached to her in the same manner that I was.

Just as I felt attachment and desire for his own mate, our minds were linked because of the bond.

He knew that I truly loved this girl, and he enjoyed watching us for his own pleasures.

Because of our bond, I didn't mind.

Though, I wouldn't ever admit any of *that* to my bride. She was so discomforted by him being present at all…

I helped her get dressed, and she gazed out at the ocean as I finished dressing myself.

"You remembered…"

I laughed. "Of course, I did. I promised, didn't I?"

She looked back at me, and I could see her eyes brimming with tears. "When are you leaving…?"

So, she knew about that…

"In the morning." I couldn't lie to her. "I will be heading to the war front after I meet with the eastern prince and his generals."

She nodded, the tears dripping down her cheeks. "I see."

I chuckled, taking her into my arms from behind, and I saw the blue of her eyes brighten as she stared at the sunset.

"I will be fine, my love," I told her. "Worry not. I am a warmongering tyrant, remember? I will be alright."

"But, I...I am not even pregnant, yet. What if something happens...?"

I kissed her tears away, noting the saltiness. "Nothing will happen, Nieves. I will be alright. In fact, I expect to not even face injuries."

She smiled. "Promise me, then."

I kneeled, turning her so that I could look up at her face. "I vow to you, Nieves, I will return as soon as I can—alive and uninjured."

She bent down, pressing her lips fervently against my own, heated and hungry for me again, and I carried her back to my dragon without missing a beat.

When we arrived back to the castle, I took her again, but I took her more gently than I had ever had her before.

She shed tears as she clung to me, letting her pleasure wash over her softly as I stroked her inside, heating her to the core.

I could have lived the rest of my life inside of this blissful warmth.

Chapter 14 – Nieves

April, 726 Fire Drake Dynasty

Tears filled my eyes as I watched him mount his dragon the next morning, his army following on horses and the few nobles that joined him on their own dragons or phoenixes.

With one last kiss and the tying of a golden and red handkerchief to his sword hilt, he had left my arms and given his princess a big embrace before he had climbed on his dragon's back and lifted into the sky as the crowd around us thundered with cheers and applause.

I didn't know when I would see him again, or if I would, but I had to trust and believe that he would return to me safely.

He had promised the night before that he would stay in contact with me via messenger hawk, so I at least could look forward to staying in contact with him.

After the emperor had left, the princess and I began having tea parties every day. Though, I hadn't expected for his departure to bring us together in this way.

Now, we were starting to really bond. I had told her a lot about my childhood, and what life had been like in the North.

We had bonded over our commonality of not having mothers, and we began to even see one another as friends.

We had so much to talk about between the two of us, and being with him had made my days special and warm. I would never allow myself to not think about how much I had grown since I had come here…

Nor would I allow myself to forget how much I truly loved this man.

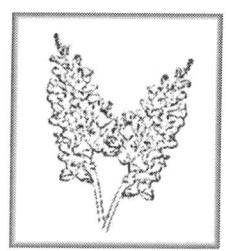

May, 726 FDD

It was almost a month after my husband had gone to war that I woke in the night to the sound of a click.

I sat up in bed, heart racing and stomach dropping for some reason...

I didn't see anything particularly ominous around me, but something pricked in my heart, something made my skin crawl...

I felt the hairs on my arms and the back of my neck stand to attention.

What...?

I was about to call out, but I suddenly felt my instincts slam in my gut to silence myself and crawl beneath the bed as the soft footsteps approached the door that joined my chambers to the emperor's former chambers.

I heard whispering and a small, dim light—likely from a lantern—as they looked around the room.

Whoever this was, they were not one of the maids and they weren't Kai...

I startled when I heard the whisper in the dialect of the central kingdom.

"Remember, King Nivia demanded she be returned alive. If you find her, do not harm her or it could cut out our reward!" The whisper was spoken in the native language of the air kingdom, but I had been studying the other languages for quite some time in order to be able to negotiate in the event of a worst-case scenario during the war.

I was suddenly thankful that I had, or else I would have no idea of their intentions.

The biggest piece of information that I had just received, however, wasn't just their intention with me; it was their *benefactor*.

King Nivia was my older brother...

Nivia had—likely in response to my husband's declaration to *not* take *his* side in war—decided to have me kidnapped and returned to the North, taking me back because my husband hadn't fulfilled the familial obligation and joined his cause.

Rather, he had joined the competition, instead.

Thus, these intruders didn't intend to actually harm me.

Likely, I would be taken back to my brother and used as a political hostage. Until something was decided, however, I wouldn't be injured.

I could count on this.

This was a team from the central kingdom, and it was likely a deal made with my brother to drop out of the war or to join their side completely against my husband and the eastern kingdom if they pulled off this mission.

I glanced from beneath the bed, noting that they were searching along the edges of the room for hidden doors. There were two hidden doors to this room, in fact, but they weren't looking in the right places.

They wouldn't find them, in all likelihood.

So, deciding to be brave with the knowledge that I wouldn't be harmed, I took a moment to calm myself first and then I stood up and quickly sucked in a breath.

"*Help*! Help, someone! *Intruders*! Intruders have come to kidnap me!" I shouted with all my might.

The intruders all jumped, stunned and in a panic as my shouts alerted the staff in the halls even as I pulled the rope to summon the maids, and I startled when my body was grabbed and thrown over someone's shoulder like a sack of potatoes.

"Let's get out of here!" He shouted. "I got her!"

They all rushed to the balcony, and I felt the wind knocked out of me as the man holding me leapt over the rail, landing easily on the back of a giant creature.

The other four intruders all landed on similar creatures, and I cried out as the palace began to fade in the distance as we fled.

"You won't get away with this," I shouted. "My husband will find me, and he will burn you all!" I snarled.

"Gag her!" The leader shouted, and the man who held me in his arms quickly forced me into submission as he tied my hands behind my back and wrapped another cloth around my head, affectively blocking my mouth.

I suddenly felt my stomach toss, and I felt like I'd be sick.

I was in for a long ride.

It was about a day and a half by air travel that we reached the north, and I was reminded of how different the harsh cold was here in comparison to the heat of my home.

Though I did enjoy the cold to a point, I already missed the warm climate of the South.

We landed near supper time, and my belly was growling harshly. I hadn't been this hungry since I had lived in this kingdom.

Would I ever get to see my home again?

It was funny…I once couldn't imagine leaving the mystical, beautiful majesty of the northern landscapes, but now, I felt like a stranger returning to this place.

Had I really spent my childhood here?

We landed in front of the main palace of the north, where my brother waited for us with a single butler and a maid.

"You found her well enough," I heard him say when I was pulled off of the beast I'd been brought here on and shoved before the king of the north.

"She didn't make it easy. She hid well, and then she jumped up and alerted the palace. I imagine there is already a thorough investigation and that the emperor has likely been alerted already."

"Hm," he said, stepping to me and taking my chin in his hand, moving my face up to look at him. "I wouldn't have expected such a thing from this little bunny," he commented. He turned my face this way and that, inspecting me, almost. "You have grown," he said. "Your skin is a little darker, and your body has filled out well," he said with an appreciative sound, appraising me. Then, he met my eyes again, looking deeply into them. "Ah," he said, a smirk on his lips. "So, I can see it in your gaze…you've been made a woman already. How unfortunate."

He let go of my face.

"…What does *that* mean?" I asked, back straight and refusing to look weak here.

He glanced at me again, an eyebrow raised. "You have learned to hold yourself high, as well. You actually *look* like royalty, now, rather than a mouse hidden away in a hole. I wonder if that will prove good or bad for me." He huffed. "What that *means*, is that I cannot sell you off to another high-born royal the way that I sent you to the emperor. You are already deflowered, so your value isn't as high. Though, who knows? Some prince somewhere may desire you more, since you've been bedded by the most vicious emperor in the known histories."

I wanted to defend my husband, but to the rest of the world, he really *was* a tyrant.

He was a terrifying, overbearing monster in his reputation.

He had earned that reputation, too.

I couldn't deny it.

I'd read enough history books and seen enough battle reports over the last few years that I knew that all too well.

My belly felt uneasy, and I suddenly felt sick again.

I felt a jolt of fear rush through my entire body, telling me to pretend I felt fine;

What if I was pregnant...?

I knew, somehow, deep in the deepest senses I possessed...if I was pregnant and my brother found out, he would almost certainly force an abortion on me.

A pregnancy would deeply complicate his plan if he did, indeed, intend to marry me off again.

If this was purely a hostage situation where I was being ransomed to my husband and negotiations made, the child would be much more valuable because it'd be the emperor's heir on the line, but if my brother intended to marry me off again?

A baby would only be an obstacle.

I needed to pretend I was fine, so that my brother wouldn't feel the need to send a physician and check me.

"What will we do with her, your majesty?" The butler asked, glancing at me with cold eyes.

"For now, keep her in the guest annex. I will see if there are any interested kings, princes, dukes or marquesses among my allies or the neutral factions who would like to marry the former empress. If not...I can try to use her to negotiate terms with that tyrant-minded beast of a brother-in-law." He shrugged. "Either way, I will gain nothing if her health deteriorates."

He turned and left, and the maid led me to the guest annex.

She said nothing as she took me to the doors, and another servant greeted me at those doors, along with a guard.

"Hello," she said. "Welcome back to the palace of the north, Nieves. You will be—"

I pulled my hand back and slapped her across the face with every bit of force I could muster, and she dropped to the ground, startled as she and the guard gaped at me in shock.

"Who are you to address the empress with such familiarity?" I asked, tone cold. "I am married to Emperor Kai Abeloth. I am the sister of your king. How dare you address me so informally and scornfully?"

"But I—"

I stepped up and slapped her again, and she bit her bottom lip as she sputtered and glared up at me.

"I. Am. The. Empress. If you don't want to face further punishment, I suggest you begin treating me with respect."

She glanced at the knight, and then back to me when he didn't rush to defend her, obviously uncomfortable and not knowing how to respond.

Finally, she acquiesced, bowing. "Please forgive me, your majesty. If it pleases you, I will lead you to the guest rooms and bathrooms, and prepare a hot bath for you after the trip here?"

I nodded. "Yes, thank you."

The rest of the evening passed without incident, but there was a lot of commotion around the castle and even the annex. I could only imagine that the news had reached my husband, and he was likely raging against the world trying to figure out who had taken me.

It wouldn't be long until he figured it out, I figured. I could imagine how panicked the staff here were, contemplating what might happen if my husband figured out my location and came to retrieve me.

I hoped that he would find out quickly, and take me from this place.

It was sad that, under the title of "hostage", I was actually treated far better than I had been as this kingdom's princess.

Painful ironies…

The night passed and soon, morning came. I didn't sleep much, too wired and restless to get any true, restful sleep.

There was a knock on the door of the annex, and I stepped into the parlor as the maid opened the door.

My brother stood there, arms crossed and looking irritated.

"Good morning," I said, dipping into a curtsy. He looked over me again, contemplating.

"My wife wanted for me to check in on you," he said, obviously not happy.

"I am fine, your majesty."

He looked me over again. "You look pale."

"I didn't sleep very well."

He grunted, looking toward the maids. "Has she had breakfast?"

"She ate a few fruits," one maid informed him. "Aside from fresh fruits, she has not been willing to eat."

He eyed me again. "You think I'd poison you?"

I shook my head. "Not at all. I've simply developed a taste for Southern cuisines…I find that northern dishes no longer fit my palette."

"Hm," he said. "I am still angry that he cut trade with us, but…the maid that cared for you in the warehouse admitted to the crime of abusing and neglecting you. She was expelled from the palace after a lashing. I realize, now that I am married myself, that I would be furious to find out my bride had been treated that way, as well." He sighed. "If he is willing to withdrawal his support for our enemies, I will release you back to him, without harming you and without selling you off to someone else. Your fate…relies entirely on him, now."

A question entered my mind. "…Who is your wife?" I asked. At his questioning look, I elaborated. "Not many people in this kingdom would ask you to check after my well-being. I was curious as to who you married…"

He looked away. "I married Lady Ava Tundra."

I gaped at him, shocked. "Ava?" I asked, stunned.

He nodded. "Yes."

Ava was my closest friend as a child. She had been close to our family, a distant relative to my mother.

Her father was a duke of our nation.

I smiled. "I am happy to hear she's well, then," I smiled. "She had always had a crush on you. I was so sad when I was locked away and couldn't see her anymore."

He nodded. "She hasn't forgotten you, either. If you like, she'd like to see you. I will send her to visit."

I nodded, wiping away tears.

That meant a lot for me. She was likely one of the only people in this country who didn't hate me.

Chapter 15 – Kai

My messenger trembled on the ground before me, begging for my forgiveness as he delivered to me the news that my wife...

My sweet, innocent, helpless, sixteen-year-old wife...had been kidnapped from our own bedchambers in the middle of the night.

Worst of all, still, was the news that we had no idea who had taken her or what their motives were.

She could have been dead, for all we'd know.

I glared at the guards I had assigned to protect her, fuming. "And you're audacious enough to call yourselves her guards?" I raged, balling up the report in my hands and throwing it to the ground. I looked to my assistant. "Make a note that I need to replace the Empress's guards immediately upon returning to the palace."

"Yes, your majesty."

I looked to my top spy, and nodded at him. "Go back to the palace, and trace the steps with the mages. We need to figure out what happened, and find out what—"

"There is more news!" One of my strategists ran up holding a scroll, still wrapped in the ribbon that would have been tied to a messenger-hawk's leg. "The messenger hawk brought this!" He said, holding it out for me.

I unrolled the scroll, reading it over aloud.

"'Have you been made aware of her disappearance yet, brother-in-law?

I am sure that the news has reached you by this point.

Rest assured; my sister is unharmed.

In fact, she is in good health.

She rests in a nice guest room and has been eating just fine. She has all her needs seen to.

She has even been reunited with a dear childhood friend who has strongly advocated for her to have proper care and has seen to her comfort here, so you can rest assured that she is not being mistreated in the least.

I imagine this doesn't give you much comfort, however.

I also assume that you want to have her returned to you, as soon as possible.

I am not opposed to her return to you, for the right price.

In return for my sister's safe return to your kingdom, I demand these concessions:

1- *You will <u>withdrawal</u> your support for the Water-Sea-Serpent kingdom of the East.*
2- *You will <u>not</u> side with the West or the Central kingdoms.*
3- *You will <u>declare your support</u> for the Snow-Wyvern kingdom of the North, and take on the West and Central kingdoms with me. Then, we shall conquer the East.*
4- *If you fail to join me, I will be forced to take drastic measures in order to secure an allegiance <u>against</u> you.*

In the end, I hope we can come to a peaceful resolution.

Signed, The king of the North.'"

What did he mean by...*drastic measures?*

I looked to my highest war-general, my most trusted advisor, Hanze. "What do you make of this?" I asked among the murmurs of my warriors.

"Hm...well, from what I heard, and how he worded it...the only thing he has that he can use to 'secure an allegiance' against you, is—"

"*The empress,*" I whispered, gaping at him.

He nodded. "Yes, your majesty."

"What does he mean by 'drastic measures'? What does he mean by 'secure an alliance against you'? I don't..."

"Your majesty," my strategist and my mage stepped over. The mage continued. "*Her majesty* would be the binding tool."

"In other words," the strategist cut in. "She will either be a political hostage to one of their enemies, likely to be killed, or…"

"Or?" I gaped, growing more and more furious.

"Or…she will be married off to one of their enemies, to forge an alliance."

I gaped between the three as things got unbearably raging in my mind.

I looked to my top advisor. "Which would you think?" I asked.

He shrugged. "Considering that they started this war against the West and Central nations, and then you joined the east to go against them because you didn't want to join their chosen opposition or join their side…he will likely try to secure an alliance rather than use her as a hostage to call off the war."

My strategist nodded. "Yes. He started war without allies in the first place, meaning that he was confident in the ability to win…that is, until *you* joined the East. When you joined the East, who was already using the war as an opportunity to attack them from the other side, he lost confidence because his enemies doubled and he had no help. If he only sent her as a hostage, it would mean the enemy could kill her if they wished, just to call off the war in general."

"He wouldn't just want to call off war, however," my mage filled in, looking at the ground as he stroked his chin. "Now that the East and South have joined to attack the North, he has to secure allies to fight against that threat. He will more than likely try to use the empress to bind his country to a new ally."

"So, what you're all saying…is that if I don't meet his demands…he will marry my wife off to someone else…?"

They all three shifted uncomfortably, and I had my answer.

"We will move at dawn," I said, noting the sun's low position. "I will retrieve her myself, and put that naïve boy out of his misery. He messed with the wrong emperor…I don't do ultimatums."

"But what about her majesty, the empress, your majesty?" My mage asked, concerned.

"She will most likely not be harmed, correct? The chances of becoming a political hostage are low. He will, almost certainly, try to use her as a binding tool, like you all said. All I have to do is retrieve her myself, right?" I asked, striding to my tent. I glanced back at all of them. *"I don't negotiate with terrorists."*

I stood in front of my army the following morning, looking over the troops.

We had only recently reached the East, and now I was having to leave to deal with something like this…it didn't bode well as an alliance partner, but the king said that he understood it.

My wife had been captured from our own home, after all.

"Today, we will lay siege to the North. Take precaution, however; *my wife* is in residence there, in need of rescue. I have been given an ultimatum, you see: Withdrawal my support from the East and join the North, or...lose my empress."

The crowd gasped and murmured, unsettled by this, and I held up my hand to get things calmed again.

"*I do not* negotiate with terrorists, and I don't accept ultimatums. We will go and rescue my empress, and put an end to this war here and now. Be warned; the North has grown powerful in their poisons and fierce in their confidence. I am sure they will be a challenge. If any of you are feeling faint-of-heart, I suggest you back out now."

There came a thunderous roar, weapons lifted into the air, and pride swelled in my chest.

My warriors were among the most loyal there were.

Even at the threat of death, they stood by my side.

I couldn't be grateful enough for these soldiers.

"**To war**!" I shouted, thrusting my sword into the air, and the army roared to life all the harder.

Chapter 16 – Nieves

"What do you mean, 'The South is moving North'?!" My brother raged, throwing the report to the ground.

I gaped at my brother from across the dining table, as he stood and paced the room, glaring at me.

"Call the knight here, now," he said, glaring at the maid. "It seems that I underestimated my brother-in-law."

"What…what are you—?" I tried, but he silenced me as he interrupted my question.

"Your *husband* must not love you as much as I thought. Rather than reaching *terms* with me, he and his forces are *marching* here for *battle*. I am sure that tyrant will lay waste to this entire place," he scoffed. "With the devastation he would bring, I'd be surprised if he even *thought* to look for you before turning everything to complete carnage."

That comment stung, but I knew that it wasn't the truth…though, I didn't refute it. I wanted him to fear Kai.

A moment later, a maid returned with a highly-decorated warrior standing there.

I could admit that he was quite handsome.

He had a tan complexion, with jade-green eyes that held hints of light brown and honey gold. His hair was a light brown color. He wore a uniform from the West…the earth nation.

"Ah, Sir Sage Terra of the Terra Marquessate, you are here. I am sure that your king mentioned a 'reward' for your loyalty and service, and that he mentioned retrieving something that would solidify our terms of peace, correct?" My brother asked, and the knight nodded, glancing at me. "Then with honor, I would like you to meet my sister, empress Nieves Eirwen Abeloth."

The knight bowed, fist over heart.

"It seems that you are being rewarded by your king for your wins in battle and your loyalty…hear me, great knight of the Earth kingdom, second son of Marquess Terra; my sister, whose marriage I am annulling due to the blatant void in our original contract, is now going to become a great uniter yet again. This time, she will unite the North and the West. I hope this time, it sticks."

I gaped at him, horrified. "Your majesty, what—"

"**Be quiet**," my brother shouted, glaring at me. "You have no right to refuse me. Your husband signed a legal, binding contract that he would take my side in the event of war; he took you as the payment for that agreement, and yet, he failed to do so when war arrived. In fact, he is on his way here, as we speak, to destroy this kingdom. *He took the enemy's side.* **He abandoned you**!" He laughed. "He voided your marriage agreement. You are now a single woman, and you are once again my property to do with as I will."

"No, you can't—"

"You are no longer empress, Nieves!" He shouted. "I am the king here, and *I* am the one in charge of you!" He shouted. "This knight was my backup plan, you see," he said, laughing.

"But I—"

"I didn't think Kai would ignore a chance to rescue you and join my side, but it seems I was wrong. Apparently, he didn't think I knew the law. Or, perhaps he didn't. He is a tyrant emperor, after all, so it wouldn't surprise me to learn that he, in fact, didn't know the law regarding marriage binding contracts. He voided it. Legally, I can proceed as I wish. Now, you will marry the Earth nation's most trusted war-general, the highly decorated captain of the knights, the second son of a Marquess…the youngest captain in their history, the genius, Sage Terra."

"Brother, you can't do this!" I cried, clutching my chest.

The knight shifted, uncomfortable.

"The papers have already been drawn and the agreement has already been made with their king. The outcome was unsure when I sent the documents to both the king and your emperor, but if your husband had only swallowed his pride and agreed, I would have blown off the king of the West and used the fallen-through truce as a provocation for further war with the west, to antagonize the earth king." He shrugged. "Now, I can just go through with this." He turned to the knight, motioning for a maid to bring the paper. "After signing this, she's yours," he said, shrugging.

The knight glanced over at me even as tears burned my eyes, sobs welling in my throat.

When I saw him and my brother sign the papers…it shattered me entirely.

"Now...take her...and *run*," Nivia said. "The emperor will be here by tomorrow. We *all* need to be evacuated by then."

The knight bowed, and approached me slowly, cautiously...a bit timid, actually.

I flinched when he took my hand, but I knew there was nothing that could be done.

I knew, from studying during my childhood and even at the palace in the South, that a divorce because of void in contract was performed on the original marriage certificate.

It was completely legal.

Voiding the terms of a contract could cause the other side to pull the plug on the marriage if he had one of the people in that marriage in his custody.

He'd had someone come and retrieve me, knowing that fact. Kai and I had never anticipated that my brother would pull such an underhanded trick...and of course, he'd waited until he knew that Kai was away because of war.

He had taken my original marriage certificate with the emperor, marked out the name of my husband with the ink of "void", a special grey-ink that you could still read the original name through, and written my new husband's name in beside of it.

Sobs bubbled out, but I swallowed each and every one that tried to escape even as my new husband took me by the hand, leading me away.

We rushed outside, out to the dark green-scaled drake with bright, vivid golden eyes with brown starbursts in the center around the pupils.

A drake was, in essence, a dragon without the wings.

He hopped on, and reached his hand down for my own even as he rumbled out speech that his drake grumbled to, conversing.

I took his hand, and he lifted me quickly to sit behind in in the saddle that was big enough for multiple riders.

We took off, the speed shocking me and taking my breath away.

I finally let it go…and I let it out.

Not caring at all what he thought, I pulled myself into his back and I began to sob and cry openly.

His large, bulky body tensed…but he didn't say anything.

There was a comfort in that, at least.

He just let me cry against him without trying to step in and stop me or bother me in any way…but I could feel him reach down a hand from the reigns and grasp my hand in his at his waist.

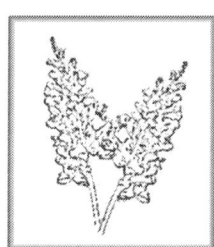

We came to a stop that night, taking a break long enough for him to hunt something small for us to eat and cooking it.

He handed me a hindleg from a rabbit off the spit, and I gingerly took a bite of it...before I rushed to the bushes, vomiting everything I'd eaten the last few days.

For the first time, I heard his voice.

"...Was it *that* bad?" He asked softly, an awkward laugh following. "I'm not much of a cook, I know, but I thought it was better than going hungry."

I glanced at him, and I noticed his warm eyes right away.

He was trying to make a joke.

I finished retching, and made my way back over to the small fire, sighing and clutching my stomach.

"I am sorry," he said, soft. "I know this all happened without your consent. I had no choice, either. I am sworn to carry out my duties and follow orders. My king ordered me to come to the North, and receive 'a reward' for my service and something that would tie our nations together as allies, to defeat the east and south. I had no idea that...*this* was what he was referring to." He bowed to me. "I am truly sorry. I saw the name voided on the certificate...you were already married. From what I see, quite happily married. I, myself, can feel your heart break. I am so sorry on your behalf."

My eyes burned, as I realized that this handsome, brave knight...had just as little control over the situation as I did.

I couldn't even be angry at him. I could blame this on him.

No...

There was only one person I could blame; Nivia.

Perhaps this knight wasn't even ready for marriage. Perhaps he had already been seeing someone, but had been ordered to come here to marry me without his knowledge or consent.

"I know this marriage is nothing more than selling you off like cattle, in your mind. I feel somewhat the same," he said, scoffing. "You don't have to like me...but I do ask that you not fight me," he said with a sigh. "I will not force myself on you, nor will I try to do anything you wish not to. I am a knight from a marquess family. I know well enough to know that the law is often unkind to women. I promise that I will be kind, courteous and protect you. That is the least I can do."

I hesitated, before I gave him a small smile. "Thank you."

He smiled at me warmly, before he started putting out the fire. "Come on, we need to get moving again. There's only a few more hours before we reach the Western kingdom."

I glanced at him sideways.

He helped me up onto the drake, and then climbed up in front of me and I wrapped my arms around him again.

He was a little bulkier than my emperor.

My emperor was muscular, but not quite as tall and broad or ripped as this knight.

He was handsome, but his looks weren't quite on par with my emperor's devilishly handsome features.

This man had a more...bear-like countenance. Stockier and larger-framed.

We rode for a couple more hours, before we slowed down, when I started clutching my stomach and the growls became loud enough to hear.

My cheeks and ears flamed in embarrassment.

"Here," Sage said, laughing, and then he was handing me a rolled-up food item I didn't recognize. "It has beef, lettuce, tomatoes, cheese, onions and peppers, rolled up in a bread-wrap. It is heavenly, and I didn't actually cook this myself. My younger brother makes these regularly, and he's a formal chef, you know."

I took a ginger bite, and it *tasted* great…

However, the moment it touched my belly, it came right back up.

We came to a jolting stop as I let go of his waist, and I quickly slid down and off of the drake, emptying my stomach into some nearby bushes.

He slid off and came to stand behind me, eyes calculating as he watched me with his hands clasped behind his back.

"…Are you pregnant…?"

I startled, gaping at him with terrified eyes, and he took that as his answer.

He sighed, pacing a moment with his hand grasping his chin.

"I see." He nodded. "I figured, when I found out you were married, that you wouldn't be a *virgin*…but I hadn't anticipated you'd already be *pregnant*. That puts me in a tough position," he said, rubbing the back of his head awkwardly as he held out a handkerchief for me to wipe my mouth and face.

I was drenched in sweat by this point. "…So…"

"That also isn't what was reported to the scouts."

"*Scouts...?*"

He hesitated. "There was a spy that your brother had planted in the South. This spy, they...um...they were...feeding you medicine to keep you from getting pregnant once you started your courses."

I froze, my blood running cold. "...What...?"

He nodded. "Your brother supposedly lost contact with them about two months ago, though," he said, thoughtful. "Or, that's what my king tells me."

"Wait, wait a moment. Are you...suggesting that my *brother* is the one who was keeping me from getting pregnant?"

He nodded. "He wanted your emperor to join his side. He thought that if he kept persuading and making offers, and if you remained without pregnancy, eventually the emperor would come around. He didn't."

Tears burned my eyes.

This betrayal...this was hard for me.

My brother had kept me from conceiving through medicine, through a spy, just because my husband wasn't abiding by his wishes?

What kind of sick monster *did* something like that?

"Are you...going to make me...*dispose* of the child...?" I asked in a whisper, preparing for the worst.

He sputtered and cough, seemingly choking on the very air he breathed at my question.

"Heavens, *no!*" He gaped at me, horrified. "Goodness, you must think me some sort of monstrosity…" He sighed, shaking his head. "I am not against your having or keeping child. I'm just…a bit overwhelmed, is all. I hadn't been anticipating getting married in the first place, and then it is thrust upon me with no prior preparation. Please, try to see things from my point of view."

"And what, exactly, is your point of view…?" I asked, soft.

"Well, I am certainly, justifiably startled. This is all very sudden and alarming and stressful. First, I am told I am coming here to receive a reward for service—not to get married. Then, there is no wedding, only the signing of a certificate before the king. Not only is my bride *forcefully* divorced from her husband, from whom she was apparently kidnapped away from…but to top all of this off, she's already carrying his *heir*…the heir of the Fire Dragon empire? The empire owned by a warmongering tyrant who is known to take up arms, invade, and annihilate entire nations?" He blew out a breath, falling to his bottom with his knees pulled up a bit, elbows resting on his knees. "It is a lot to take in over a *day*, you know. I'm only *twenty*."

I sat beside of him. "Well, to be fair, I'm not even *entirely* certain I'm pregnant, yet. If I am, it is very, very early. I didn't even know, but had only just started to suspect it. My brother would have had no idea. Neither would Kai."

He gave a nod, considering that. "I see."

"Could…could Kai even reclaim the child?" I asked, genuinely asking. "I mean, *we* are legally married now, aren't we? I probably cannot even keep his heir away from him. That wouldn't be right."

He gaped at me. "You are asking about the same tyrant that the rest of the world is terrified of, right? You want to find him and offer him his child, but *you* remain with *me*? Simply for legality's sake...? Are you insane? You expect him to just *leave* you with me?" He asked, looking almost amused. "I'll be lucky, indeed, if I even make it out of this alive."

I smiled. "Don't worry. Even if Kai comes for me and the baby, I'll protect you if you've been good to me."

He laughed, holding out a hand for mine. "You mean, the legendary tyrant is actually loving to someone?"

I nodded, serious. "Yes. He is...really quite sweet. You should see us together. You would think that all o the rumors of him are false. Goodness, you should see him dote on the princess, even. It is funny, how sweet he is. He would listen to me. I promise, if you are good to me, I'll protect you."

He gaped at me, before he gave me a warm smile. "Then, I'll take you up on that deal, your majesty," he said, bowing his head to me.

I shook his hand, and he helped me to my feet and dusted me off before we mounted his drake again. Then, we continued onward...

To the Earth Drake kingdom.

A few hours later, we had arrived to the city.

Thankfully, it was late in the evening and there was almost nobody around.

We were able to make it through the check in at the gates to the city and through the streets to his large mansion in the upper ring of the city without seeing many people at all.

Those we did see paid us little attention.

When we arrived to the mansion, he slid off and, taking great care, helped me slide down easily into his waiting arms.

A butler came out, bowing.

"Welcome home, master Sage," he said. He glanced to me. "Might I prepare some tea for you and your guest?" He asked, smiling at me.

"Please ask the cook to prepare something to help with nausea, and bring some herbal tea for the mistress of the mansion."

"Very good, my lord—*mistress?*" He asked, gaping at me.

Sage nodded. "She is my wife, as of today."

"M-my lord, that is *very* sudden—"

"It was by order of the king. An arranged marriage, to reward me for my services and to bind the West kingdom to the North kingdom."

The butler gaped at me as I lowered the hood of my cape that Sage had put over me earlier in the evening, before we'd reached the city.

"It is good to meet you," I smiled warmly at him, giving a slight curtsy.

He appraised me for a moment. "Your manners...they are *perfect*," he looked at me in awe. He glanced to Sage. "Might I know my new lady's name?" He asked, looking back to me.

"I am Nieves Eirwen Abeloth—well, Terra, now..."

The notebook he'd been holding slipped from his grasp, fumbling to the ground. He startled, rushing to pick it up. "Ab-*Abeloth*?!" He cried. "You mean...are you—" He looked at me. "The *empress*?"

I nodded. "My brother forced a divorce between the emperor and I due to voiding our marriage contract's terms, before he married Sir Terra and I..."

Sage shrugged, sighing. "Yes...it was quite sudden, for the both of us. For now, please just retrieve what I've requested, and have the maids begin preparing the Madam's suite. Oh, and Slate—be sure not to tell *anyone* about her true identity. To everyone but you, she is simply Lady Terra. Do you understand? The last thing we need is gossip running rampant. Be *beyond* discreet."

The butler bowed. "Of course, my lord."

"Also, I need you to contact a doctor—someone reputable but who knows how to keep their mouth shut."

"Yes, my lord," the butler said. He bowed before he scurried away.

Then, he turned to me. "I will have you examined to be sure that you are doing alright, and then...then, we will sit and talk."

I gave a nod. "Alright."

I was shown to the parlor to wait for a bit, along with some tea, before I was shown to the dining room to have a meal with Sage.

After about an hour, and having had our small meal, the butler had returned with a physician.

She confirmed my pregnancy and was paid extra to remain silent and discreet about the ordeal, before she had left and all of the servants had been sent out for the night.

I sat at the dining table across from my new husband, and he rested his chin on the back of his clasped hands, eyes calculative.

"What is it that *you* wish?" He asked suddenly. "Were you...*happy* with the emperor?"

I nodded desperately. "Yes!" I said, sincere. "He was very good to me. He was kind and considerate, and the only thing he put before me at any point was his daughter...but even then, he made sure that I wasn't in the wrong first before he said anything or did anything. There was once that she tried to frame me for attacking her, for example. He was ready to kill me if I had, but he proved my innocence and punished her instead. Since then, he has always come to me first to ask me."

He considered this. "You love him, even after something so scary."

I nodded. "Yes."

He sighed, shaking his head and grasping his hair. "I don't know what to do, here," he said. "I have been ordered by our king to take you as my wife, and at my *rank*...I am but a soldier, who has gone from being a commoner to gradually climbing the ranks to become nobility through my military service. I have sworn fealty to the king. I cannot go against his orders, lest that make me a traitor. But I don't want to see you unhappy and miserable, either." He groaned. "What am I supposed to *do*...?"

I glanced down at my clenched hands. "I am sorry to put you into this position..."

He smiled. "It isn't your fault. Your brother is the one to blame for this. He wasn't getting his way, and he went against your will and kidnapped you from your husband. He even dissolved your marriage. Now, we discover you are with child...the emperor's child. When he finds you, all hell will break loose, you realize?" He asked. I nodded, and so did he. "You are positive that you want to go back to him?"

I nodded. "I do."

He sighed, soft. "I cannot *directly* go against my king. I can't even set up help for you, or I risk their lives and my own." He thought about it. "Give me tonight to think about this, and I will come up with a plan."

I nodded, before I was led back to my own chambers and I finally fell into a restless, long-suffering slumber.

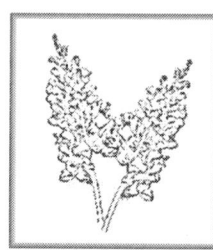

The next morning, it was about three in the morning when I was shaken awake and motioned to be quiet.

"We're getting you out of here," he whispered, soft. "All of the servants are finally asleep, and the guards are shifting posts around the city. It is the only time we have. We have about an hour."

He rushed to get me dressed, and get me a back-pack and a horse ready. He told me, as we rushed to get me going, that there was food and provisions, as well as nausea medication, inside the pack.

He mounted behind me on the horse after he got the pack into place, and we began to ride.

We reached the outer part of city rather quickly without gaining any attention, and then he dismounted the stallion and pressed a kiss to my hand.

"Get out of here. Here is a map, and we are here," he said, pointing it out on the map. "Follow this road, and it will lead you through the forest and back to the South. Ride quickly, and keep your face and hair hidden if you can. I pray that you are able to reach him."

"Thank you," I said, leaning down and pressing a chaste kiss to his lips. "Thank you…"

He grinned up at me. "I will try to act like you are just staying holed up in your chambers for a day, to try to give you a little time. Try to get as far as you can before then. I won't let anyone figure out that you aren't here for as long as I can." He held out a long dagger, and strapped it to the saddle. "Take care of yourself."

I nodded. "I promise, I'll repay this, someday." He smiled and nodded, and then…then, I was out of the city and into the forest.

I passed a few travelers on the trails, but I kept my head down and passed on by without a word.

It was starting to get dark, when I heard something that made my skin crawl.

It was a group of knights, looking to be dressed in the uniform of an enemy of both my brother and of my emperor.

They leered at me, cat-calling and whistling.

"Hey, there, pretty lady! What's a fine young thing like you doing out in these parts without a man?" They called, riding their horses after me.

I didn't respond, and that made them angry.

Nausea began rearing its ugly head as I tried to ride faster.

"Hey," the ring-leader shouted, looking upset. "You know it's rude to ignore someone when they're talking to you?"

Fear spiked in me, and I nudged my horse onward faster, despite the roiling of my stomach and the lurching of bile up into my throat.

Even if I began to vomit, I would not stop.

"Hey!" He shouted, and they charged toward me.

Tears burned my eyes, and I cried out when they caught my horse in a lasso and I nearly fell off.

"She's got a cute cry," they laughed and hooted, and dismounted their own horses before dragging me off.

I grabbed the dagger's hilt and jerked it out from its sheath, slashing it at them.

I managed to cut one's cheek, and he glared at me a look that burned in its intensity.

"You...marked...my...face...?" He asked. I had to admit, this one had been handsome. I imagined that he won the affections of many women with that face, so this would make him exceedingly angry. "Oh, this cunt is mine," he said, and the others backed off. He swung at me, a harsh slap to my cheek, and I startled and shouted out in pain.

He pulled me to him, and within moments, he had me down to the ground as his group looted my things from my bag.

"You're lucky I don't do worse than this," he slapped me again, and busted my lip.

Tears ran down my cheeks in rivets, but I held my sobs in. Bile held in my throat, and I started to feel like I was choking.

Still, I forced my glare to remain in place.

If being the wife of a tyrannical emperor had taught me anything, it was that you should do your best not to show weakness.

I couldn't stop the tears, but I could keep my cries bottled in.

"Oh, look what we have here. Tough girl, hm?"

I felt the wind shoot out of me as they ripped off my dress with force, and I glared at them as they all leered and ogled me.

As they laughed at me, I cringed when their hands touched me, and I couldn't just sit and let this happen.

"You should stop, now, before you perish!" I shouted, putting as much power in my voice as possible. "I am the wife of the Tyrant, and if you have any sense, you'll let me go before he finds out what happened and kills you!" I shouted.

They stopped, looking amongst each other before laughing.

"Then I guess I'm about to fuck an empress," the leader smirked at me, before he freed himself from his pants.

Then, he shoved himself into my mouth, grunting and spouting out lude nonsense.

This...this vile beast was shoving himself into my mouth while the others hooted and whistled!

Pigs, the lot of them.

No, they were worse than pigs. "Pigs" was both an insult to pigs, and a compliment to these savages.

I did the only thing that I could think to do—I bit down as hard as I could, and I did my best not to gag as blood filled my mouth and he screamed, shoving me away as hard as he could.

I hadn't severed the penis from his body, but I had severely injured him—to the point that it was partially severed, and it would have to be cauterized.

Good.

I stood, and as the others rushed to help *him*...I bolted.

My blood pumped as my heart raced, and I dashed through the forest with all that I had.

"Kai!" I cried. "I just want my Kai!"

My pleas fell on deaf ears, but I could hear the others catching up to me.

They sounded like they were back on horseback, which was bad for me.

I was on foot.

Sobs tried to rise out of my throat, but I kept them pinned down.

There was no way they would let me live after that…

"Help!" I shrieked, praying beyond hope that something, someone, somewhere, would hear me and come to my aid.

Suddenly…I heard something I hadn't heard in a long time.

I heard the shriek of a young wyvern.

I froze, looking up to the skies, and I saw a sight that I'd never have imagined before.

I saw a beautiful adolescent wyvern, that was white with glittering gold and red scales over its body and stunning silver eyes.

I'd never heard of such a coloring for a wyvern before.

I didn't know how I knew, but I was desperate, so…I spoke to it. "Help me! Please!"

Only, I didn't speak it in any human tongue I'd ever heard, and my entire body burned as I realized that.

The wyvern barked out a shrieking call in response—

"**Yes**."

Then, it swooped around in a circle before coming in to land, even as the knights finally caught up to me, shouting and cursing me.

"Please, protect me from them!" I cried to the wyvern.

It glanced at the knights, and I watched as its throat glowed a bright blue before it blew out snow and freezing wind on their feet, freezing their horses in place before the throat glowed yet again.

This time, it glowed red…and I watched, mesmerized, as it set them all on fire and incinerated them in moments.

What…?

No known hybrids had ever existed.

A drake inheriting two elements had never been known or seen.

How was this even possible?

When the area was clear and I was safe, I turned my attention back to the wyvern.

It approached me, looking over me with a calm and contemplative face.

"Who…are you?" I asked.

Again, my speech was not humane.

"I am Burning-Wind," he spoke, the voice obviously male. "I have waited a long time for you."

"You…but I…"

He gave me a look over. "Your blood is sickly. Did your parents die of sickness?"

I gaped at him.

My mother had died of complications just after giving birth to me. Had she actually been sick?

Was that part of the reason that I'd been the way I had?

Was I sick?

"My mother died just after I was born. Nobody ever knew the reason."

"It is a genetic disease. Perhaps that is why I had to wait."

"But why would you have to wait?"

He cocked his head. "A noble must be strong enough for the bond. You were not so until this point, because I have never smelled or sensed you before."

That made sense, but I could not understand the reasoning behind this.

"What is your name?"

"I am Nieves," I said. I glanced around. "Can you...take me home?"

"Where is home?"

"The South."

He gave me an annoyed look. "South..."

"What...?"

"I don't like South," he grumbled. "Dragons are stronger than me. I am stronger than the wyverns."

"Ah," I grinned at him, looking him up and down. "A wyvern after my own heart. You would like my husband."

He was a stunning creature.

"Is he the father of your hatchling-to-be?"

I laughed as I climbed up onto his back. "Yes," I said. "He is the emperor of the South…"

"That tyrant is notorious," he grumbled again, irritated. "His dragon is one of the strongest in the world, and the strongest one in active service to a master."

I made a mental note of that.

He suddenly pushed into the air once I had gripped onto his spinal spikes, and I gasped as the wind knocked out of me when we took to the skies.

I laughed and felt freer than I ever had.

How had I gone so long past my coming-to-power age without this?

How had I survived without him?

Tears stung my eyes as joy and relief blazed through my heart.

Burning-Wind.

I clung to him and let myself feel safe for the first time in a while as we flew South.

Chapter 17 – Kai

"***Where is my wife*?!**" I bellowed as I held my brother-in-law by the collar, even as his wife was held in the grip of one of my generals with a knife to her throat.

"Sh-she's already been married off!" He finally admitted after two times of asking me. I'd only just had his wife grabbed for the third time asking as a threat. "She...I sent her to the Earth—"

I punched him in the face as hard as I could manage, and though my hand throbbed, I felt satisfaction when his cheek busted open from the force.

"You stupid, stupid child!" I scolded. "Rip up the contract. If you don't want to lose everything you have—because I was so generous as to leave your castle and your kingdom intact and come directly here—then I will revoke that choice. Rip up her marriage contract entirely. She belongs to me, and we both know it. Do this, and I will spare your lives."

He cringed, but with a glance to his wife, who gave a desperate and quick nod, he sighed and ordered it to be ripped up.

"The marriage contract is null and void," he said. "Now, please...leave my home..."

I shoved him to the ground. "You no longer have a sister. Forget that she ever existed. Never contact her again, or I. Will. End. You."

He nodded frantically before I turned and strode out.

"We head west!" I shouted.

It took two days to reach our destination, and this time, I didn't just go directly to the king without fighting anyone and being peaceful.

No. This time, I had my army incapacitate every single soldier by knocking them out, doing my best not to fatally harm anyone so that Nieves wouldn't think me a monster.

We made our way up the streets toward the castle, and within a few hours, I was standing before their king.

"Emperor Kai Abeloth," he acknowledged. "To what do I owe this honor?"

"I'm sure you already know…that the wife your soldier received was *my wife*."

"Ah," he said, a knowing smirk on his face. "So, can you continue to ignore the—"

"I've already defeated your soldiers, who are all unconscious. I have come for my wife. The marriage contract to your soldier was marked as null and void and destroyed, and thus, she remains my own."

"Oh, dear," he said, looking annoyed. "So, the young king of the north couldn't hold out, hm?" He sighed. "Fine. Take it up with her husband, then." He gave me a map, pointing out the address. "Though, I wouldn't bother. The girl ran a few days ago."

"...What...?"

He shrugged. "Appears that she wanted to go back home. She had been gone an entire day before it was noticed." He sighed. "Too bad. She was a looker. Though, from the way that I hear it, the soldiers who tracked her down found traces of a dragon attack and left-over loot lying around. I think a young dragon must have caught her, probably."

Fear speared me, but I strode out and to the husband's address.

It didn't take me that long to reach, as it lay not far inside of the city's gates.

When he ushered his servants out of the way and bowed to me, eyeing me up and down, I could see in his calm and happy face that he hadn't touched her.

"Did she make it to you?" He asked.

"...What?"

"I helped her get out of here," he said, quiet and looking around. "She wanted to go home to you, so I gave her a horse and supplies and sent her to go home. She found you, right?"

"...No."

"What?" He asked, upset. "But I—" he paused. "Oh, I...I hope she's okay. I had hoped that what the other soldiers told me wasn't true. But she might...she might be..."

"She's not dead," I said, refusing to believe that. "Thank you for helping her." I tossed him a giant sack of gold coins.

"You..." I paused, and turned to him. He scratched the back of his head. "You really love her?"

I smiled. "Yes."

He gave me a grin back. "*She* really loves *you*, too. She told me so. That...that's why I helped her escape. I was ordered to marry her, so I had to do it secretly, but...I don't believe in forcing a woman against her will. She has someone she loves. Even if you're my enemy, I know that I would want someone to let *my wife* return to me rather than keeping her against her own will."

I nodded. Enemy nation soldier or not, I could see that this was a good man.

That made me contemplate, morbidly, just how many "good men" I'd killed who could have been loyal soldiers to me, instead.

"Thank you. I appreciate that." I turned, then I made my way back out of the manor and to my dragon.

When I reached my group, we made our way back out of the kingdom, and into the forest.

We followed the horse-hoof prints through the path, and after about half a day, we found giant scorch marks on the ground, as well as items such as a pack and swords and shields scattered about.

My dragon let out a huge huff, and I turned to him.

"What is it, Flame?"

"She's been here. There was a fight, and then...something came."

"...'Something'?" I scoffed. "Can you be more specific?"

"No," he huffed, irritated. "I do not know this scent. It smells...unfamiliar."

That wasn't something I'd ever heard him say before. He always knew what the smells around us were, from animals to even the distinct races of people.

He always knew.

"Something that Great-Flame doesn't know?" I asked, surprised, and he gave me a withering expression at my use of his full name.

I mounted him, and I glanced to my general. "Send a message to the palace, and ask them to keep an eye out for the empress. I will make my way home and see if I can find her that way."

I had my dragon take to the sky, and follow the smell. If any creature had laid waste to my empress, I was damn sure going to make sure I saw it suffer before meeting a justified demise.

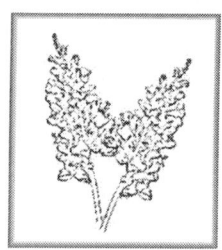

Days of searching passed, and there was no sign of her. The scent of the...oddity had disappeared, and there were no visible signs of her.

Word had gotten back from the palace that she hadn't returned, but that my idiotic advisors had gone—behind my backs—and brought in a noblewoman from our own empire to become my bride.

Enraged, I decided that I'd had enough.

As the only named Emperor on the continent, of these united kingdoms, and the ruler of the most powerful of the drake types...

I decreed that I would be taking over then entire continent.

Any and all kings had to declare their support of my general rule of the continent.

They could remain the representative for their own respective kingdoms, but they would be reporting directly to me, and they would follow my laws.

Any and all who chose to go against me would perish.

It was time for me to become the dictating tyrant that everyone saw me as, and take back what was mine.

Nobody was taking me seriously enough, it seemed. They would regret having ever crossed my wrath.

I would only spare those who could prove to me they were innocent.

Fuck it all.

Chapter 18 – Nieves

May, 726 Fire Drake Dynasty

It had been a while since I had been back here, but it *smelled like home.*

The servants all gaped and gasped when I landed at the landing pad for the dragons in the courtyard, and I smiled at the butler as he rushed out with a panicked expression.

"Hi, I—what is it? Tell me what's wrong." I asked when I noticed his face.

"My lady, what...*what* are you doing back here?"

"What...?" I asked. "Well, I...I escaped the western kingdom, and I've returned home—"

"Madam, you *can't* be here!" He rushed me, glancing around in concern. "The new empress won't allow it!"

Everything in me stopped. I could feel my heart stall almost.

"What?" I choked. "New...*new empress...*"

"They brought in a new empress for his majesty!" He cried. "She's ordered that if you are found on the grounds, that you be brought to her for execution!"

"Has she been coronated?" I asked.

"Well, not yet, but—"

"No," I said. "There is no '*but*'," I told him. "Unless she has been formally and officially coronated with the emperor himself, then she is not the true empress. The council cannot do that without the emperor and his authority."

He paused. "You are right, madam, but…"

I patted him on the shoulder. "Don't worry. I am the last coronated empress, and I have returned."

"*You have no authority!*" I heard a voice screech, and I looked over at the doors that led out to the landing pad.

There, of course, stood *Faiza*…the same noblewoman I'd had issues with before.

Of course, it would be Faiza.

It had always been Faiza for the counsellors. They had always favored her, desired to have a "home-bred" noblewoman as the empress.

She was from a good family and powerful bloodline, with good society connections—such as, her "friendship" with the princess.

Arms crossed, a sneer on her face. "As the reigning empress, I demand that this vulgar foreigner be sent to the prison!"

Soldiers rushed out at me, and grabbed me.

"I am sorry," they murmured to me. "Until the emperor returns, we don't know what to do…we…we all know about the marriage dissolvement. Even if she isn't coronated, yet, your marriage to his majesty is technically dissolved, legally."

Damn.

I had been hoping that they hadn't found out about that.

They took me into the palace and through the halls before we reached a metal door, and then we went in and down the stairs that led to the dungeon.

I was taken to a cell and left there, and I sighed as I sat down.

Several hours passed until I was taken by the guards and brought *back out* of the dungeon.

What...what were they doing?

What were they planning to do with me?

Was I going to be expelled from the empire?

They led me out to the ceremony space where one would get their dragon, and there was a stone table sat up now with a place for my head.

Wait...

Were...were they going to...

No...

Surely, they weren't going to behead me!?

"What are you doing?!" I shouted. "I've committed no crime! You cannot execute me without reasonable cause without the emperor!" I began to struggle, but Faiza came and struck me across the face.

"You've brought this upon yourself, you know. You should have known your place. The butler even gave you an out, the fool! Speaking *of*—" She motioned for him to be brought forward, and I gaped and watched in horror when the soldiers forced him to his knees at the block. "Kill him."

Maids were crying, and tears stung my eyes as I watched the executioner bring down the headman's ax and cut off his head.

I cried out, remembering my friendship with that butler, and I mourned.

"How...how could you kill him just for trying to help me? You *monster*!"

She shrugged. "I demand absolute obedience, and *I* am the new empress. Once you are out of the way, Kai will have no choice but to accept the decision—and accept me into his bed," she sneered at me. "Bring her forward!" She laughed.

"No!" I screamed, struggling.

Something...anything! I had to think of something!

Then, it dawned on me, and though I had wished for it to remain a secret for a while longer, I had no choice.

I would have to use my one and only card to play. "I am the harbinger of the emperor's child!" I shouted. "I carry the emperor's child within me! You *cannot* kill me! Bring forward the physician to confirm it for yourselves! If you kill me, you would be killing the emperor's heir with me!"

The council immediately rushed to stop the execution, rushing and clamoring around me and arguing with the empress even as my wyvern screeched.

"Burning-Wind" I cried.

Gasps and screams filled the air as blasts of wind so cold that it felt like they were burning shot out at those around me, and I rushed to get out of the way and off to the side.

"*Burning-Wind!*" I cried again, and he looked my direction, coming to me quickly as dragons began to reach the area. "Quickly!"

"We *can't* harm her!" One advisor shouted out. "If she's truly pregnant, we've been waiting for this for *years*! The emperor *must* have an heir! She is the last *coronated empress*! Stand **down**!"

"*Give me that!*" I heard a shrill screech, and I glanced behind me to see Faiza yanking a bow and quiver of arrows from a guard before she notched one on the string.

I cried as it grazed my arm, and my wyvern shot out a fireball at her.

She dodged as her dragon landed in the area behind the group, and I rushed to my wyvern as she conversed with her dragon loudly and with anger.

I felt my stomach churn as fear roiled through, and I gasped out as I reached my wyvern, clinging to him and trying to crawl up onto him.

"*That is enough!*" I heard a voice boom, and I almost fell to my knees in relief.

Kai!

Kai had returned!

Everyone dropped to their knees, kneeling to the emperor, and I hid behind my wyvern as Faiza continued shooting arrows in my direction.

"***I commanded you to stop***!" Kai thundered, and she gaped as she finally noticed his arrival when his dragon landed overtop of her own, almost double the size.

"B-but I—" She tried. "I am the empress! I am your new wife! She's just a dissolved marriage, a—" She tried to finish, but he slapped her.

She looked on, dumbfounded as she held her hand to her cheek.

"*You* are *nothing* to me. The marriage dissolvement form was burned and turned *null*. Nieves is still my legal, coronated empress. You have just committed treason!" He shouted.

"*No!*" She cried, gripping his arms in her hands, digging sharp fingernails into his biceps desperately. "I am empress! *Me*! I was always meant to be your wife!" She screeched.

He backhanded her this time, knocking her away from him, and she sputtered and gasped as he strode to me with confident strides and pulled me into his embrace.

"Nieves," he murmured into my ear. "Did I hear that right? Is it true?"

I blushed, but I gave a timid nod. "It is true," I said, soft.

A smile I'd never seen before spread across his face, and he absolutely beamed at me. "I'm going to be a father?"

I nodded. "Yes..."

He hugged me tightly, but around his shoulder, I could see Faiza notching another arrow.

I gasped, pushing him out of the way at the last moment.

"Kai!" I cried…

Then, everything went black.

When I awoke, I was lying in bed, with a doctor and my husband and step-daughter at my side.

"She is indeed pregnant, and the baby seems to be fine. Just be sure that she rests and gets plenty of peace…her risk of losing the baby is higher if she is active and busy."

"I will be sure she remains calm and relaxed," Kai said, shaking his hand. "And the wyvern?"

"Bonded to her and confirmed as her companion," he told Kai. "I don't know *how* they found one another, but he is hers and she is his."

"Right," he said. I could hear the smile in his voice. "That is good."

"She finally got a companion, daddy?"

He chuckled. "It would seem so. I wonder why it took so long."

"He told me…that I was sick. My mother…apparently died from a hereditary disease," I said, and they gasped and rushed to my sides.

"Mother!" Conlaed cried, burrowing her face into my side. "Thank goodness you're okay!"

I gaped down at her. "…Mother…?" I asked, and my husband chuckled.

"She's felt guilty since you were kidnapped, for not being better to you. She promised that if you made it back safely…she would truly treat you as her mother."

Warmth tingled my heart and belly and tears burned my eyes.

"Oh, goodness," I said, soft, hugging her. "There, there. I'm alright."

"Are you dying, then?" Kai asked me, looking worried. I shrugged. "You don't know?"

"Burning-Wind said that I would probably need medicine, but that if I could get that, then I wouldn't die. He said it is curable. They just…must not have known my mother died from it. They always thought that my birth…was what killed her."

He gripped my hand in his, and smiled sadly at me.

"I am so incredibly thankful that you made it back safely."

I smiled. "I gave it my all. Did I do well?"

"Yes," he chuckled. "You did very well. Good work," he told me, hugging me. "The palace sorcerer came and told me to bring you later to the laboratory, and he would determine what gender the baby is whenever we are ready," he grinned at me.

I smiled. "We can find out this early?"

He laughed. "There isn't much that the sorcerers cannot do," he admitted.

"I am excited to see what the baby will be, but also...I need to do something, my love," I told him.

"What would that be?" He asked. "Tell me anything, and I will do it for you. I'll give you anything."

I smiled at him. "Yes...I know."

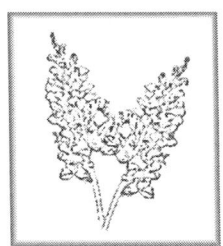

August, 727 FDD

"Come on, now," I laughed when my child slapped my wyvern's snout. "Don't be mean to Burning-Wind!" I said.

"He seems to like the wyvern," I heard a voice laugh out, and I turned.

"Sage!" I grinned, welcoming my personal guard.

The request that I had made that day?

I had begged for Kai to hire Sage from his kingdom, and bring him in as my personal guard.

He also arranged for a good woman to marry him, in honor of his loyalty and kindness to me, and he was an expectant father-to-be, now.

"Sorry it took longer than I thought that it would," he beamed, holding up a tray full of sweet cakes.

I rubbed my swelling belly, rushing to take one off of the tray and eat it before I gave my son a tiny piece.

"Conlaed, can you take the prince for a few minutes?" I asked her, and she rushed over to me and took her baby brother.

After I had awoken all those months ago, Kai had executed the advisors had brought in a "new empress."

Then, executed Faiza for treason, and taken over the entire continent as the only official ruler.

Within record time following that, he had brought in Sage to be my guardian. They were on good terms as friends, too, and so he trusted me with Sage. Of course, Sage had more than proven himself.

It was interesting to see three different drake types together, though.

It had taken a while for Burning-Wind to get used to life in the South, but now he was good friends with Kai's dragon, and he was searching for a mate for himself now that he was reaching adulthood.

Burning-Wind and Flame both struggled to get along with Sage's drake, but they were coming along.

Prince Zane Abeloth had been born in November of the year 726 FDD, and the entire palace adored him.

It was simply impossible not to.

He had his father's dark tan skin tone, but he had my white hair and my storm-like grey-blue eyes.

Conlaed had absolutely fallen in love with being an older sister, and spent much of her time helping me to take care of him—completely voluntarily, ready to pitch in and help. She enjoyed it, and he adored her. He was always smiling at her and excited to see her.

I was now three months pregnant with a second prince, according to the sorcerer, and Kai was just beside himself with excitement.

Kai was an excellent father, always doting on us and always jumping right in to help.

The first few nights of having a baby had been tough for me. I had so bonded to Zane during my pregnancy, that I could hardly stand to even have the staff look at him without feeling like I wanted to gouge their eyes out…which was a completely foreign feeling to me.

Taking care of an infant, however, required help that I wasn't mentally prepared to receive.

The first few nights, when Zane had cried for me, Kai had leapt out of bed and jumped into action. Changing the baby's diapering, cleaning him, bringing him to me to nurse and letting me sleep while I did so as he would sit behind me and hold my arms around our son firmly into place.

Then, he would take our baby back to his crib, and lay me down to sleep comfortably before coming back to sleep himself.

During those early days and even still, our dragon and wyvern would take shifts resting on top of the palace, just over-top of our balcony, to protect from intruders on that side…just in case.

I'd had quite a bit of post-traumatic stress over that for a while, constantly wary and afraid to sleep because I thought someone would sneak into the room from the balcony and kidnap me or hurt my baby…

Kai had finally brought me enough reassurance that I could sleep soundly ninety percent of the time, now, and I was increasingly ever-thankful for him and his care for us.

The children and I shared the sweet cakes, and I laughed and joked with Sage even as we watched the children play silly "peek-a-boo" games.

Life was good…and I loved every moment of it.

February, 728 FDD

"*This will be our last,*" Kai insisted, looking me in the eye when I awoke. "It took four sorcerers to heal you and bring you back from the brink of death, Nieves. There will be no more for us."

Tears ran down from my eyes, but I gave a single, gentle nod.

I would concede on this, for the children's sakes.

"Ishaan and Kiran," I told them. "Prince Ishaan and Princess Kiran."

Conlaed meant "Chaste Fire."

Zane meant "White as snow."

Ishaan meant "The Sun."

Kiran meant "Ray of Light."

Prince Ishaan had my skin tone, orange-toned red hair that was a little lighter than his father's, and his father's burnt-orange eyes.

Princess Kiran had skin that was a little more tanned than my own, but not by much. She had my white hair, but her father's burnt-orange eyes.

Together, there were four children between the two of us, Kai and I.

August, 729 FDD

Just as it had been tough with Zane, it was a struggle with Ishaan and Kiran. This time, we needed my maid to help us with their care during the nights, as we still had to take care of Zane during the nights, as well.

I spent a lot of time crying, struggling for reasons that I couldn't fathom.

Even after a spell that rendered my uterus useless—until the spell was removed, anyway—the emotions and endless waves of mourning hit me over and over.

Kai tried desperately to fix it, wondering what in the world was wrong with me…but I couldn't even think of anything.

I had spent months crying on end, struggling to get out and about…

Finally, one day, Kai had enough of it.

He set it up for Sage and Conlaed to watch the children, and he led me out to our dragon and wyvern companions.

We mounted and lifted to the skies, and he laughed when I gasped as the wind was knocked out of me.

It had been so long since I had ridden…

We raced, laughing and cutting up, and tears of joy burned my eyes as I spread my arms out like wings, closing my eyes and just...being.

When I looked to my husband out beside of me on his dragon, he was watching me with a completely blissed expression.

"What?" I asked in a laugh.

"Oh, well, I just haven't seen you so happy in so long," he grinned at me. "Seeing you like this...it is exactly what I hoped for."

I smiled sheepishly. "You've been so gracious with me," I admitted as we came to land in a clearing in the forest. "You've been so patient."

"I just...I remember when I lost you," he admitted. "When you were taken, and I learned of what happened, I felt like I would die. I broke, and I realized just how much you meant to me. I vowed to myself that if I was able to bring you back safely, I would never hurt you. I wouldn't push you or leave myself to regret even a single moment of our time together. I would know that I had done everything in my power to do right by you. There are already things that I regret in the past, and I knew that I didn't want anything else on my conscience to feel bad for. I determined to be the best husband that I could be for you, Nieves."

Tears ran down my face, as I pulled him down to kiss me.

"I love you, Kai," I whispered.

"You are my everything, Nieves. You have given me everything." He kissed me again. "Happy birthday, Nieves."

I jolted. "Birthday...?"

"You are twenty years old today," he laughed. "Now, look around."

I did, and I gasped when I realized.

We were surrounded by snapdragon flowers…all red and orange, but with a single, gleaming white one in the center of the field that you could tell had been planted there.

I was breathless. "K-Kai…"

Then, he pulled me into his embrace. "I remembered you telling me about the single red snapdragon you found in the field of white ones in the north. I even found it, myself. So, I brought a white one here and planted it for you…"

"Oh, Kai," I murmured. "Thank you." I blushed as he began to strip me and love me in our usual way.

It was the best birthday I could have asked for.

Epilogue – Conlaed

February, 732 Fire Drake Dynasty

It was my eighteenth birthday, and I was drinking a glass of wine when a thickly-accented, warm male voice spoke to me.

"May I think it would be your honor to dance with me?"

I turned, seeing a man around my age, and I glared at him. "Excuse me?"

"A lady from the South, yes? I like women with spicy attitudes."

"No, thank you," I said, trying my best to maintain my manners the way that my mother had taught me.

He gaped at me, and gripped my wrist in his hand. "How arrogant! I like feisty women," he said, licking his lips.

I went to slap him, but he caught my other hand easily and held me.

Why had I gotten off to myself to drink? I sincerely regretted it, now.

"I said, 'no'," I reiterated. "Or did your mother not teach you the meaning of that word?"

"You shut your mouth!" He shouted, and I flinched as he moved to slap me…

Only, the hit never landed.

I opened my eyes to see a stunning, gorgeous man standing there.

He had dark, charcoal-grey hair and deep, dark blue eyes.

"The princess said 'no,'" he told the man.

The man gaped at me. "P-princess..."

"I am Conlaed Abeloth, the eldest daughter of Emperor Kai and Empress Nieves," I said. "You have committed a treasonous act. In my mercy, if you leave the palace now, I won't kill you," I said.

He barreled out of the hall, nearly knocking over a maid, and fled the scene.

"Well done, princess," the new, handsome stranger spoke. "Well handled."

"I...suppose that I should thank you," I said.

He shrugged. "I only did what I felt that I should. I have three younger sisters, and I wouldn't want them to have to deal with such a thing," he laughed.

"I-I see," I smiled, tucking some of my hair behind my ear. "Well, thank you, um—?"

"I am Navy Riverian. I am a duke of the Eastern Sea-serpent kingdom. And you are the daughter of Emperor Kai," He chuckled as I opened my mouth to reintroduce myself. "You are a lovely lady, your highness."

I blushed thickly. "Thank you..."

He bowed at the waist, and held out a hand for me. "May I have a dance, your highness?"

I smiled. "Yes," I told him.

I let him lead me back to the ballroom, and we danced.

Over the span of the next few months, he and I would grow close as my mother insisted that he be allowed to stay in a special annex on the estate, and soon, he asked my father for my hand in marriage.

When my father asked for my opinion, I all too happily begged him to accept the proposal, and within eight months of meeting and courting…Navy and I were husband and wife.

Thanks to my mother, I actually did know a little about the first night…

It was just as magical as I had hoped it would be, and I was prepared when I felt sore the following day.

Over the next few years, we would struggle with fertility.

By the time my younger brother, Zane, was reaching his coming-to-power, however, I found myself pregnant.

I would give birth to a son, who would succeed his father as the duke. He had been born with his father's dark grey hair, my dark tan skin, and my bright golden-toned eyes. He would remain my only child…but at least he would have lots of cousins to play with!

Zane would grow to marry General Sage's eldest daughter when they turned seventeen and sixteen.

Ishaan would marry a woman from the fire-drake empire named Firetta, and together, they would have three sons and a daughter.

My only sister, Kiran, would grow to marry a man from the western earth-drake area, and they would have one son and a daughter.

My father and mother enjoyed their time together, with the hatchlings of their dragon and wyvern becoming companions to my siblings, and they spent their days roaming the skies and making love.

They were the couple I looked to for what I wanted my relationship to be like with Navy.

I couldn't fathom having a better relationship than what they had, and I knew...I knew, instinctively, that nobody would ever love as much as my father loved my mother.

Bonus Chapter — Burning-Wind

July, 278 Fire Drake Dynasty

I huffed in my spot, as the emperor's dragon flew around on his break while the emperor waited on the rooftop with me.

We listened to my mistress crying in the bedroom, racked with some inner demons that made her cry all of the time.

She swore that she was happy, but she just cried and cried and felt miserable even though she was happy.

She stayed stressed, begging for mercy…but mercy from what?

"What can I do for her, Burning-Wind? Nothing helps her. What even is wrong? How can I fix things if I can't see anything to fight?" He sat curled with his knees to his chest, arms folded overtop his knees and looking out at the sea. "How can I fight something unseen? I can't just leave her with no support, either. I want her to rely on me, but what is she fighting?"

"The sorcerer said 'post-partum depression,' right?" I asked, and he nodded. "Perhaps she needs a day of fun and relaxation away from the children, with no responsibility. Remind her that she is everything to you, and that she can come to you. I have noticed her pulling away lately."

"But why? Why pull away?" He asked. "I've done all I can to show her that I'm here, that she and the babies are my priority—"

"Maybe she needs to know that this time…just *she* is your priority. Make sure she knows that you are here for her."

He contemplated this.

"I think that I know what to do…"

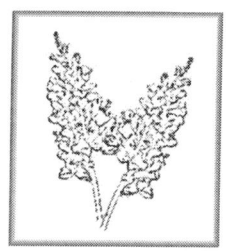

September, 239 FDD

Ten years went by in a flash, and Nieves did get better over time.

It had taken some time, but he made sure to make time for her. He made sure to show her, prove to her that she was his love and priority.

He made sure that she knew that he was there to support her, love her, and be there for her, with no judgment and no shame.

He took as much pressure off of her as he could.

After their special outing, I watched the emperor cultivate their bond and love her with his entire self.

He made sure that she knew that she came first and foremost in his mind and heart, and that not even the children would fall before her.

It took quite some time, but eventually, she became completely at ease and at peace in her life.

I watched over her and my hatchlings and enjoyed my life, and when she passed away many years later—at the age of eighty-nine—I would remain by her grave, guarding her for the remainder of my days.

Her children and grandchildren and great-grandchildren would visit often, and I imagined that she was happy with all of the company.

The emperor had died a few years before she had, and the throne passed to Nieves' eldest son, Zane, and then his eldest son and so on.

It remained peaceful as time passed, until war arrived amongst the dragons and other drake subspecies.

It was really a needless, senseless turn of events, in my opinion, but there was simply nothing to be done.

It became a turning point in history.

One of the Master Dragon's hatchlings had been unjustly murdered, and it had turned to all-out war.

I chose not to do any fighting in the war, but the former emperor's dragon did, and he had been rather upset at me that I had not joined his subspecies to help.

It had almost ended our friendship, too.

Still, the war ended up involving all of our kind, while I just wanted to rest and remain by my master's graveside.

I knew that I couldn't forever avoid the war, and that I would die at some point, but I wanted to remain true to her until the very end...no matter what.

I was about three-hundred years old when my time came, and I was killed by an Earth Drake who was young and strong.

At the very least, I'd led a peaceful life, and I knew that my mistress would welcome me into the bliss of the heavens when I passed from this earthly plane.

I would find later that I was right…

She did.

Family Tree – Kai Abeloth

(DIRECT LINE ONLY)

Crimson Abeloth + Heather Storm – **Asher Abeloth**
|
Asher Abeloth + Thistle Stone – **Kindling Abeloth**
|
Kindling Abeloth + Amara Sands – **Wick Abeloth**
|
Wick Abeloth + Cinderelle Blaze – **Kai Abeloth**

Kai Abeloth + Ashley Blaze – **Conlaed Abeloth**

Kai Abeloth + Nieves Eirwen – **Zane Abeloth**, **Ishaan Abeloth**, **Kiran Abeloth**

Family Tree – Nieves Eirwen

(DIRECT LINE ONLY)

Glacian Eirwen + Niviana White – **Glacier Eirwen**
|
Glacier Eirwen + Purity Storms – **Tundra Eirwen**
|
Tundra Eirwen + Neveah Byur – **Stormy Eirwen**
|
Stormy Eirwen + Icy Tundras – **Glacial Eirwen**
|
Glacial Eirwen + Nevis Eirwen – **Nivia Eirwen & Nieves Eirwen**

Nieves Eirwen + Kai Abeloth – **Zane Abeloth, Ishaan Abeloth, Kiran Abeloth**

Extras: Name pronunciations and descriptions:

(ALL images used were referenced from Google, just a general base I used to reference character appearances, and can be found on Google.)

Nieves Eirwen: Nee-ehh-vehss, Ay-uhr-whehn. 5'3", pale, white hair, stormy-blue eyes

Name: Nieves Eirwen
Rank: Princess, Empress
Faction: Part Knight, Majority Mage blood
Mage Mana inferior
(DISCLAIMER: found on Google, these are not my images)

Kai Abeloth: Kye Ah-beh-lahth. 6'2", dark tanned, muscular, orange-auburn red hair, burnt-orange/red eyes.

Name: Kai Abeloth
Rank: Crowned Prince, Emperor
Faction: Majority Knight, Part Mage blood
Knight Aura superior
(DISCLAIMER: found on Google, these are not my images)

Conlaed: Cahnn-layed. 5'3", dark tanned, orange-auburn red hair, golden eyes.

Zane: Zayyn. 5'10", dark tanned in the book, white hair, storm-blue eyes.

Ishaan: Ee-shahhnn. 5'8", pale-skinned, orange-auburn red hair, burnt-orange eyes. (No image to insert)

Kiran: Kee-Rahnn. 5'2", light tanned skin, white hair, burnt-orange eyes. (No image to insert)

Sage: Say-j. 6'. Tanned, muscular, brown hair and golden hazel eyes.

Fin

We hope you enjoyed The Royal's Saga, Book 3:
The Disregarded Dragon
Please join us for the next installment of The Royal's Saga:
Book 4: The Hidden Queen…

Book Excerpt to follow

Kinley

June, 506 Lawrence Dynasty

"But why do we have to move again?" I asked. I didn't understand why we had to move around all of the time, why we couldn't stay in one place.

"You're the one who decided to take your blindfold off!" My father shouted, and I felt something strike me. I yelped, cowering. "You know better! You can't take off your blindfold. You are not allowed to see."

"I don't—"

"I don't care that you don't understand. You need to listen and obey, and that's all you need to know. If you do that, you'll stay fed and sheltered."

Pain radiated through my arm where what felt like a boot had struck me, but I lifted the shoe and tried to sense my way over to my father to return his shoe to him.

He grumbled, but took it, and I held onto my rope that kept me tied to the wagon as we began walking again.

Father said that the wagon was pulled by the horse, and that it held all of our things so there was no room for us to ride on it.

It wasn't a large wagon, but I felt his presence leave my side even as I kept walking along and I had to think that he was, in fact, riding on the wagon.

For as long as I could remember, I wasn't allowed to use my eyes. I didn't know what anything was, or even what colors were.

The two occasions that I had taken off my blindfold, I had been so overwhelmed that I'd almost immediately closed my eyes and felt blinded.

The last time that I had taken it off, however, we'd had one of father's friends over, drinking with him…he had seen my eyes before they had closed, and there must have been something bad about them because just like the first time I'd opened my eyes, we'd left that same day.

I remembered feeling suddenly surprised and happy when I had met that man's eyes. He was thinking that I was special.

Though, I didn't see how that was possible, when father insisted that I keep my eyes covered. Perhaps they weren't special. Maybe I was scary?

Father kept most of our belongings loaded on the wagon at all times, just in case.

In *this* case, the man had begun crying out and shouting in alarm, and father had demanded he leave before he grabbed me, carrying me out to the wagon and tying me to it before we left our small little shack.

Father worked small odd jobs as a carpenter, so he could work anywhere.

Whenever we met new people, he told them that I was his servant girl, and I guessed that he must be ashamed of me because I couldn't use my eyes.

If only I had been normal.

He also regularly dyed my hair, so I assumed that he hated my appearance entirely.

I didn't know where my mother was, or what had happened to her. All I had ever known was *this* man.

Perhaps...perhaps, I mused in my mind, my mother had died or had left my father on bad terms, and left me with him.

He seemed to strongly dislike me.

I didn't know how to ask my father for information, either.

We found lodgings just after dark. I knew, because I could see the vague change of lighting through my blindfold and my closed eyelids, no sunlight filtering through to my vision.

"Alright, we'll stay here for the night. I have to go inquire about a job and housing tomorrow, so I need for you to stay here and out of trouble."

I gave a nod. "Yes, father."

He grumbled, but we got our horse tied up in the stable before we entered the building, and we were led upstairs to a room.

"Goodness, when is the last time the girl had a bath?" A lady asked. "How would any lady like to be around you if you can't even take care of a young girl's hygiene? She *stinks*," she commented. "I can give her a bath, if you like."

He grunted. "I guess she could stand a bath," he said. "But don't mess with her eyes. She's blind, and sensitive to touch around her eyes."

We stepped into the room, and the woman got me a spare dress and a towel—or at least, that is what she told me that she was doing, before she led me to a room off of the main room. I heard the water filling the tub before she helped me undress and helped me feel my way to the tub.

"Where are you two coming from?" She asked, making conversation. "We don't see a lot of slaves in this area."

"S...slave?" I asked.

"You're a slave, aren't you?"

"No," I said, soft. "That man is my father."

"*Father?* You don't look anything like him, miss. He has rich, dark, chocolate skin, and you have white skin. Did he *tell* you that he was your father?"

I hesitated. "Well..." Come to think of it...he hadn't. Not once had I ever heard him say that I was his daughter, or call me his daughter to me, myself. I shook my head. "Actually...*no*. I've just always been with him. He raised me. We move whenever someone sees my eyes. Oh, but he's so good to me and takes care of me," I said, trying to defend him against her harsh tone. "He even feeds me his extra bread and scraps, and he lets me eat mushrooms and fruits from the woods when we travel."

She paused. "Why..." I suddenly felt the girl take off my blindfold. "I'm going to wipe your face," she said, and I felt a warm wetness on my face as she got my face and neck clean. "Can I see your eyes?"

I quickly shook my head. "*Nobody* can see them. That's why we move so much."

"But you're in the middle of a move, aren't you?" She asked. "I won't tell anyone."

"Well…"

"You don't have to be scared. You can't see me, anyway."

"I *can* see," I said. "But something is wrong with my eyes, that's why they stay covered."

She hesitated for a long moment, something thick hanging in the air, and I tensed. She seemed to know more, and I wondered if she knew why my eyes stayed covered.

Finally, she spoke to me again. "May I see? Please? I'm sure they are beautiful! You are such a pretty girl."

I…*I was pretty?*

I'd never heard that before…

"What does pretty mean?" I asked, and I felt her shock.

"Well, it means a good thing. Pretty is good."

I mulled it over for a moment. If she thought that I was pretty, and pretty was a good thing, and she promised not to tell anyone about my eyes…it wouldn't hurt to let her see them, right?

I slowly opened my eyes; the light stung, and she quickly moved the lantern a bit further away to let my eyes adjust.

The first thing I saw was her bright hair. I didn't know the color, but it reminded me of heat, for some reason. The strange color that filtered through my eyelids when the sun was setting, a burning color.

"What is that color?" I asked, looking at her hair.

She startled. "You...you *can* see..."

"I can see," I noted. "I told you. But I've never seen that. I don't know what that is."

"My hair is an orange-red, miss. I am named Ginger, for my red hair."

I noted her dark skin, and her bright eyes. I felt a sudden rush of surprise, the breath leaving me.

What...what *was* this?

It didn't feel like *me*. I didn't feel surprised, so where was the surprise coming from?

"Why do I feel so shocked?" I asked, alarmed. "I feel so heavy," I said. "I...I feel surprised, and happy, and I—" I suddenly felt fear, and I met her eyes again. "W-what's wrong?"

She jumped, eyes wide, and I felt a rush of fearfulness.

"Are...are you okay?" I asked, and she stood.

"You...you're the missing...you're the..." She hesitated, rapidly shaking her head. "Never mind. I must be wrong. It couldn't be. Your hair isn't the right color."

"Well, I don't know what you mean, but father dyes my hair."

She gasped dramatically in horror, before she hurried to finish bathing me, and she got me rinsed and dried off.

"Don't...*don't* repeat what I said to your father. You are beautiful, and have very pretty eyes. Don't worry miss, I won't hurt you or tell anyone. You can trust me." She tied my blindfold back in place, and helped me into a new set of clothes and out of the bathroom.

My father wasn't around, and I was glad, even as the girl—Ginger, she had called herself—quickly took her leave, letting me get into bed.

I was the missing...*what?*

I felt lost.

Was I a missing whatever I was?

Had father...?

Was I...*kidnapped?*

I supposed that it would explain why he was so harsh with me sometimes, but I thought he was just a stern father.

Was he...not really my father?

Her words played back in my head. He had dark chocolatey skin, and I had pale peach skin. How did that mean that we weren't related?

Did skin color need to be similar to be related?

I didn't know anything about these things!

Though, I supposed that if I looked nothing like him, that must mean that we didn't share relation. What did that all mean?

Sometime later, I was getting myself curled up on the pile of blankets that I had found on the floor, where I assumed my father wanted me to sleep.

I hadn't ever slept in the bed with him, and he had always told me that kids were supposed to let the grown-ups have the bed, because as your body ages, the floor isn't tolerable anymore. I had to sleep on the floor while I was still young enough to handle it.

I heard the door open and shut hard, and I flinched against the irritation that I felt entering the air.

"Here," he said, and I startled with a small moan when something soft suddenly landed on my lap.

It smelled delicious, though! I took a deep breath, and brought the softness to my lips, taking a bite of the bread roll that he'd given me.

It was the first I had eaten today, and I was surely hungry!

"I'm going to bed early tonight," he said. "We will set out as the sun rises, so get to sleep quickly. We need to get out of here," I heard him say gruffly.

He was in a bad mood.

Had someone made him feel urgent? He sounded urgent…

I saw the light through my eyelids go out with a huff from him, and I assumed he had put out the lantern. I heard the bed shift, and I tucked myself on my blanket as best I could.

I waited and waited, on the very brink of sleep when I noticed his breathing change, and he began to snore.

I…I wanted to know.

I wanted to know, for sure. Was he not my father?

I took my blindfold off carefully, and I let my eyes slowly adjust to the darkness.

There was still a lantern lit in the corner of the room, so that he could see if he had to go use the bathroom, but it wasn't very bright. It was on a low setting, obviously.

I stood, and tiptoed over to the edge of the bed, peering at the only companion I had ever known, and I startled at what I found there.

There lay an incredibly dark-skinned man, with black hair that was thick and curly.

She had been right. We didn't look even remotely the same.

My skin was a pale, pale light color, and I knew that my hair was white because he had told me so. So, my skin was almost white.

I glanced at this man, feeling suddenly like he was a complete stranger.

Had I really spent all my life with this man who looked nothing like me? Did everyone think that I was a slave?

I knew that he told people that I was a servant, but a slave?

Was that his intention with me?

Why did he, exactly, keep a girl around who he seemingly disliked who wasn't allowed to even use her eyes?

What was the point?

I startled when I saw a light outside the door, and a few shadows as hushed voices whispered outside our room.

I glanced around, panicked. Were they here to hurt us? Rob us?

What should I do...?

I quickly put my blindfold back on even as I heard the clinking of keys, and I rushed to the edge of the bed, shaking my "father."

"Father!" I said in a frantic whisper. He roused right away.

"Wha-what? What?" He asked.

"There're voices outside our door, and something clinking…"

He startled, leaping up and swooping over to peer at the door—I assumed. I felt the breath nearly knocked out of me as he whisked me up into his arms, and I felt a rush of cool night air as he opened the windows.

I gasped as he jumped out of the window even as we suddenly heard the door of the room burst open, and he slid down some bumpy hill—I guessed the roof of the inn.

I clenched and sucked in a deep breath, feeling my entire body sinking as we fell, and we landed with a hard thud and he took off running.

"Father, what's going on?" I asked, alarmed.

"Shut up, girl. I need to focus, I don't have time to answer your nonsense right now," he said quietly as raised voices started to get closer. "Shit!"

We took off in the opposite direction, and I felt him shove me up onto an animal. From the snorts, it sounded like a horse.

He quickly unlatched its restraints, and jumped into the saddle behind me before we took off, and he commanded the horse as we rode, fleeing.

That seemed to confirm things well enough.

If I wasn't in danger, or if I wasn't kidnapped...those people would have had no logical reason to invade our room at the inn, nor pursue us.

Fear struck through my entire body.

Was I in danger?

What was I supposed to do, now?

...

.....

....

....

.........**Want to keep reading?**

Be sure keep an eye out for the release of
The Royal's Saga, Book 4: The Hidden Queen!

It only gets better from here, and let us not forget: STEAMIER.
...Y
U...
...M

Books by Kristen Elizabeth

The Royal's Saga

The Apathetic Knight, Part 1
The Apathetic Knight, Part 2
The Villainous Princess
The Disregarded Dragon
The Hidden Queen
The Conquering Empress
The Abandoned Prince
The Decoy Duchess
The Empathetic Brother
The Anonymous Writer
The Luxurious Slave
The Royal's Behind the Scenes Finale Novella

The Shifter's Saga

The Rejected Lady Book 1: Parts 1 & 2
The Rejected Lady Book 2: Parts 3 & 4
The Hunted Cat
The Damned Wolf Parts 1 & 2
The Justified Siren
The Lost Heirs Parts 1 & 2
The Trapped Son
The Shifter's Behind the Scenes Finale Novella

The Lover's Saga

Titles coming soon!

The Spell-Caster's Saga

Titles coming soon!

The Dreamer's Saga

Titles coming soon!

The Queen's Saga

Titles coming soon!

The Knight's Saga

Titles coming soon!

The Immortal's Saga

Titles coming soon!

The Villain's Saga

Titles coming soon!

The Children's Saga (PG13)

Titles coming soon!

Acknowledgments

A special thanks to my proof reader, Trisha, for reading through the novels and helping me with the grammatical and spelling aspects. Without your help, there were a lot of mistakes that would have made it into the books.

A special thanks to those who supported my work, including but not limited to Trisha, Sammie-Anne, Shannon, Amber, and so on. Several people who really encouraged me to write, publish and seek higher things. You guys inspired me to make this possible. I appreciate it so much. Special thanks go to my most avid of fans, including Christine, Jeanna, and a few others who had been following my work and have gone to extra measures above and beyond to support and read my works. All of you aforementioned people make writing the books so much more exciting so that I can see your reactions and give you good books to read! Thank you all for being amazing. Without you, there is no way I would have gotten such a great start!

A special thanks to my husband, Reece, for allowing me to take so much time to write and keeping everything running yourself. You knew how important it was to me to be able to write and complete my works, and you didn't get angry about it. You were always understanding and pushing me to publish the work. You wanted me to pursue my goals, and I needed that extra push because I'm bad about procrastinating on things. I love you, handsome ;)

Lastly, I want to give a special thanks to my mom. You don't even read my work, but you encourage my writing and creativity even if you might not agree with the content. Thank you, and I love you.

About the Author

Kristen Elizabeth is now on social media! Follow on Instagram and Tiktok! Handle for both apps is (lovelymadness92) Follow for more bonus content, updates, and publishing schedules!

Kristen is a stay-at-home mother to two special-needs boys and wife from North Carolina who comes from the rural country, and grew up in a broken home. The daughter of a single mom who tried her best and worked multiple jobs to keep a roof over their heads.

Kristen spent the majority of her life emersed in arts and music, and used writing and reading as an opportunity to escape from the trauma and depression that spiraled out of control from the abusive background she crawled out of.

Writing, arts and music opened up an entirely new world for her, and she kept herself surrounded by it to avoid the stress and anxiety that was forcing down on her.

Kristen, herself, is also on the Autism Spectrum, and wants to share her unique worlds with those around her. She doesn't think she's all that special, but hopefully, someone out there will enjoy her creations as much as she does and use her creations to escape from the mundane everyday life.

Kristen's biggest goal is to fit somewhere outside of the norm, and to broaden horizons in the world of fiction.

Life isn't always happy endings, sunshine, and rainbows.

Sometimes, life is an utter freakshow and things don't work out the way you hoped.

That's something that Kristen wants to bring to her writing.

Kristen intends to take a couple of months off, after the rapid publishing, and spend that time working on the next books, marketing, promoting, etcetera.

None of this happens without the readers and fans, and any and all sharing and spreading the word means so much to me!

Thank you to all of my dear readers,

Kristen Elizabeth

Made in the USA
Columbia, SC
21 May 2023

16541283R00165